Praise for *Counted Worthy*

Every generation must discover its own storyweavers. Leah Good is one of ours and we are fortunate. *Counted Worthy* is a thrilling work of inspirational fiction that perfectly complements the message of *Do Hard Things*. Grab a copy for yourself, grab a copy for a friend, and help spread the word about this phenomenal debut. *Counted Worthy* belongs in the hands of every Christian teen and story lover in the country. It's that good.

–Brett Harris, *author of bestselling Do Hard Things*

This is a timely novel during a year that international persecution of Christians has regularly made headlines.

–Woody Robertson, *co-founder of CollegePlus*

Counted Worthy is quite possibly the best contemporary Christian fiction I've ever read. The strong, beautiful message is clearly conveyed without the slightest bit of preaching; something exceedingly rare in today's Christian market. The premise, both unique and familiar, shines like a candle in the dark, forcing you to re-evaluate just how far you'd go with your faith. Ultimately, it instills a desire to follow God to the end of this world. Eagerly awaiting Miss Good's next novel!

–Catsi E, *reader*

Radical. Intense. Compelling. Leah Good's dystopian novel, Counted Worthy, powerfully embodies the me~ 'hat today's young people need to hear: the Rea~~ lie to self, pursue the impossible, and w'⊥ This is the message that has the ~ placency into a generation of i.

~, *reader*

Intense. Even if you ~~, you can still find appreciation, inspiration ... wait in anticipation reading this novel.

–R. Stars, *reader*

Counted Worthy

Leah E. Good

Published by Leah E. Good
P.O. Box 4421
Wallingford, CT 06492

ISBN 978-0-9913245-1-4 (pbk.)

Layout: Penoaks Publishing, www.penoaks.com

Printed in the United States of America

10 9 8 7 6 5 4 3 2 1

Dedicate To

My family.
Mom, Dad and Jonathan, thank you for encouraging
me and making this novel possible.

Yu-Ming and Yuhua Chang.
It is an honor to have grown up knowing this faithful
couple who stayed true to the Lord despite persecution.

My Lord and Savior.
May everything I write be dedicated to honoring and
serving Jesus Christ.

Chapter One

I sat back on my heels, picking at my black nail polish and waiting for the single, bare light bulb to flicker. A normal teenage girl would never work her full shift if she could help it. Especially a full shift at this job. Most teens thought processing books at the government sorting center marked the apex of dullness.

I glanced towards the camera that blocked most of the tiny basement window. I preferred to keep working, but I wanted to look normal in case someone was watching the security screen.

The red Bible in my peripheral vision tempted me to give it my full attention. What kind of idiot made a Bible red? Anyone who saw it would pay attention for sure. Not a desirable quality for a Bible. If I didn't nab it now, it would end up in the incinerator for sure.

I gave up my effort to look bored and snatched a romance novel with an embarrassing front cover off the pile of paperbacks. I saw worse at school every day, but the cover still bothered me. The art of wearing enough clothing and keeping it on had died sometime before the Great War. These days even our teachers encouraged the stupidity.

I flicked dust off the barcode and swiped the book across the in-wall scanner. "Acceptable." Go figure. One more disgusting book would re-enter the world while the quality ones burned. If only there was a way to get Christian literature into the hands of ordinary people. It would change the country.

I sighed and gave the rest of the novel a slap-dash wipe with my rag. It would never happen. I tossed the romance novel into the sales bin.

The light flickered just as the book thumped against the other acceptables. Sunset. A few seconds of darkness before the batteries kicked in. My window of opportunity. I slipped the Bible off the pile. The binding threatened to crumble as I slid the little book into a secret pocket sewn into the lining of my leather jacket.

The light came back on, steady this time. Dust and flakes of red pleather stuck to my hands. I wiped them on my rag and dumped the cloth down the trash chute. Time to go home.

I jogged up the stairs and flipped the light switch off. The smell of book mold stayed with me. I hoped the manager wouldn't notice.

"I finished stack C." I scanned my student card to clock out. My name and age popped up next to my picture. Heather Raziela Stone. Sixteen years old. I tapped "correct" on the screen and called a little louder, "I'm going home."

The manager straightened from behind the front desk and peered over her glasses. "Find any banned books?"

The edge of the little Bible poked into my ribs. "No, ma'am. Not today."

"Good." She lifted her eyebrows in what passed for a smile. "I think after all these years we've finally burned most of them."

"Maybe." I slouched, waiting for her to let me go.

Her head dipped forward. She ended every conversation the same way.

"Have a good evening." I forced myself to walk slowly and give a casual, over-the-shoulder wave.

The arrival beeper chimed as I pushed through the front door. I let the door swing behind me.

Dead streetlights lined the road like sentinels and offered no light against the gathering dusk. I walked close to the buildings, my black clothing concealed by the shadows.

The crisp spring air nipped at my face. April should be warmer, I told myself. I zipped my jacket to my chin and shoved my hands into my pockets. Conscious of the other people on the street, I maintained a careless swagger. Anyone who noticed me would see a Goth teenager. I prayed they wouldn't suspect anything more.

Storefronts gave way to private houses as I distanced myself from the cluster of businesses and government outposts. My work took me too close to the border of the main city. I preferred my outdated but less claustrophobic neighborhood.

The overgrown shrubbery covering the windows of my house looked spookiest at this time of day.

Neighborhood kids dared each other to venture onto our property on All Hallows Eve. The rest of the year, they steered clear. It worked well for our purposes, but I wished we could keep people away without making our house look like the set of a horror movie.

I poked my head into the garage. Dad's bike was missing, which meant he was working late again. My bike leaned against the far wall. Even from a distance, I could see a layer of dust on it and the way the tires flattened out on the bottom.

I turned away from the bike and made sure the garage door clicked behind me. Someday I would live in a house without so many ghosts.

As I stepped onto the lawn, a cool breeze off the lake behind the house blew my hair into my face and made me shiver. I circled the house, ticking off a mental checklist as I went. No broken windows, no forced locks, no torn up grass, nothing out of the ordinary.

Reassured, I took a deep breath and allowed myself to relax. The smell of damp earth and flowers made me smile. Maybe tomorrow I'd cut some daffodils for the kitchen table. Dad would like that.

I fished my house key out of my pocket and let myself in the side door. The familiar scent of Dad's aftershave and our government-issue, all-purpose cleanser greeted me. I relocked the door and slipped my shoes off.

Two steps forward, a shuffle to the right. I groped for the battery powered lantern hanging on its peg, and found it easily. The routine was as natural as tying my shoes.

I flicked the lantern on and headed for the kitchen. On the table, the salt shaker held down a yellow scrap of paper. Dad's big, almost illegible cursive scrawled across it.

Heather,

You must still be at the Sorting Center. They need me back at work. Don't worry, I ate. Hope you had a good day.

Love, Dad.

I slipped the note into my jeans' pocket. Just like Dad to waste a precious piece of paper when he could message my screen. Nothing could train him out of his old habits.

The blue-tinted glow from the lantern reflected off the window. I pulled the shades down. No point letting strangers look in and see me home alone.

The Bible bumped against my ribs like a little kid making sure it hadn't been forgotten. I patted it and headed for the windowless hall. One forbidden Bible— or even the suspicion of a forbidden Bible—could cost me my life. I knew that truth better than anyone, but I couldn't stop going back for more.

I settled cross-legged on the floor and set the lantern next to me. The Bible stuck to my sweaty hand as I removed it from my pocket. Dust from the cover swirled in the soft light.

Red. Vibrant, brick red. So strange. Things that broke the norm meant trouble more often than not. We'd have to rebind this Bible before we gave it to Ansley.

I rubbed my finger over the faded gold lettering on the spine of the book. *Holy Bible: Red Letter Edition.* My heart fluttered. No matter how scared I got, no matter how hard I tried to repress it, the excitement over finding a Bible never lessened.

Ansley, one of my friends in our underground church, had given her Bible to a new family just last week. This one would replace hers.

I started flipping through the pages and frowned as some stuck together. Sometimes that happened when we bound or rebound a Bible. Could this one be brand new? A Bible from before the war that had never been used?

The fake leather kept flaking onto my hands as if protesting the very thought of being new. I slapped my palms together and stood up.

As much as I loved Bibles, I never felt safe with one in my hands. Still, I didn't envy normal people. The way they lived made them miserable from the inside out. I only longed for one aspect of their existence. Their lack of fear. I wanted to experience that feeling.

I went to my room and slid the Bible beneath my mattress. It nestled between two other old books, the titles almost unreadable. *Do Hard Things* and my own Bible. My babies.

After Mom died, my books kept me grounded. I had distanced myself from the people and activities that had once filled every free moment. I cut as many ties to the underground network as I could. I attended church because conscience compelled me. I continued to smuggle Bibles because I couldn't help myself. Everything else, I shoved into the past. I filled my free hours and aching heart with books. They still felt like real friends.

I lowered my mattress. For now, these precious volumes would remain safe.

As I readjusted the blankets on my bed, a key rattled in the front door. I listened as the door creaked open.

"Is that you, Daddy?" I headed for the kitchen.

"It's me." He sounded tired. I could hear him hanging his coat before coming into the kitchen. He dropped a stack of papers onto the table.

"Still working?"

"Still working." His brown hair spiked in odd places, a sure sign of stress.

"You need anything?"

"A hug and a kiss would be good." He opened his arms to me.

I hurried to hug him, smiling as his strong arms squeezed the air out of my lungs. If books were my friends, Dad's arms were my place of safety. His hugs warmed my heart.

"You're squishing me," I mumbled into his shirt.

He let go and kissed my forehead. "How was your day?"

"Good." I looked up at him, waiting for his next question. He always knew how to read me.

"Your expression gives it away, sweetheart." The tiredness in his eyes faded a little as he smiled.

"Do you want to see it?"

"Of course."

When I came out of my room, Dad stood in the hall holding the light. We swapped. He ran his fingers over the Bible, read the spine, then opened to Proverbs and tilted it towards the light.

"You did a good job." He smiled, but his eyes didn't light the way they normally did when I found a Bible. "You're a brave girl, Heather. Your mother would be so pleased with what you're doing."

"Dad, don't." My breath caught in my throat. Why did he have to travel this path over and over?

He looked at the Bible and stayed quiet for a long time. The loneliness for someone we couldn't have thickened the air between us.

Dad looked up. "Would you do it if I weren't here?"

"Are you going away?" I skirted his question. Leaving meant either arrest or going into hiding. I didn't want to face either possibility. I hugged my arms to my chest and stepped back.

"I didn't say that." Dad's voice stayed steady. His job as a screen entertainer on regional live cast forced him to stay calm, cool, and collected in front of an audience. He applied the talent with equal skill in his private life.

"I don't know," I said. It was a neutral but honest response. A response that avoided the snake's nest of emotions threatening to bubble up. Dad couldn't leave. I needed him. *God, do you hear me? I've lost enough.*

Dad sighed. "Police came snooping around the office today. It's not the first time. They keep singling me out and asking questions."

I looked at the floor to avoid Dad's searching gaze. Fear wrapped its icy claw around my chest. Why would they single Dad out for questioning if they didn't suspect him? What had we done wrong? Was it my fault?

I will trust, and not be afraid. The verse surfaced as an automatic response to stress. Those words linked my thoughts to all the hard times in my life. It had been my support, my verse of refuge. Now it carried a mix of comfort and pain. *God is my salvation; I will trust, and not be afraid: for the Lord Jehovah is my strength and my song; he also is become my salvation.*

A tear escaped and started down my cheek. I scowled and ducked my head.

"Sweetheart." Dad slid a finger under my chin and tipped it up.

I forced a smile.

"We don't know what they're looking for," he said. "They might not know anything."

"Maybe."

Dad set the Bible next to the lantern and reached for me. I leaned my head against his chest. The tears pooled until I couldn't hold them back. They slid down my face, leaving wet circles on Dad's shirt.

I clung to him, not wanting to let go. What would I do? How could I live without him? Maybe I was blowing the situation out of proportion, but I couldn't stop my mind from scrambling to achingly painful possibilities.

When Dad stepped back, I hurried to dry my face. Black mascara smudged onto my fingers. Pathetic.

He squeezed my shoulders. "I won't run away if they come for me. What will you do if that happens?"

"If you're taken?" I stared at the floor. "I don't know."

I looked up and found an expectant expression on his face. He wanted me to sound spiritual, but I only felt scared.

"Think, sweetheart. What will you do?"

I closed my eyes and drew a deep breath. What would I do? My eyes still closed, I let the air out in a rush and settled on an answer to satisfy both of us.

"I will fight the good fight," I said. "I will finish my course. I will keep the faith." I opened my eyes. "I don't know beyond that."

Dad smiled and, for the first time that night, his eyes sparked. I loved that expression. It transported me back to carefree childhood days when his smile could set my world to right.

"That's all you need." He held the Bible out to me. "Our lives are but a vapor."

I took the Bible from him and nodded. "But the word of the Lord endures forever."

I clenched the Bible until my hands ached. These pages held the words of life, but how many would have to die to preserve them?

I jolted awake and sat up in bed. Someone pounded on the front door, demanding that all occupants of the house present themselves. The police. Or, more likely, The Agency. The special division of the police force often pounced on its victims by cover of night. They preferred to attract as little attention as possible.

The door to my room flung open.

"Up," Dad hissed. "Hurry."

I scrambled out of bed and lifted the mattress, groping for the two Bibles and *Do Hard Things*. I found them and pulled them from their hiding place.

"You know what to do," Dad said. I couldn't see him, but I sensed his presence near the foot of the bed.

I snatched a hoarded plastic bag out of my nightstand. The plastic crinkled in my shaking hand. No number of drills could fully prepare me for a moment like this. The rush of adrenaline made me dizzy.

I clutched the books to my chest.

"Dad, come with me." My voice wobbled and cracked. I knew it was a useless plea. He wouldn't run. If he came with me, the police would continue their search. Dad would never endanger me that way. Why did he have to be so stubborn?

Dad crossed to me and pulled me against him. He kissed the top of my head. "Go, sweetheart."

The pounding on the front door turned into a rhythmic smashing.

"Dad, I can't."

His hand lingered on my face for a moment. I felt a flicker of hope. Maybe, just maybe...

He shoved his Bible into my hands, and the moment passed. "He hath said, I will never leave thee nor forsake thee."

"Daddy." I wanted to cling to him. My heart pounded.

"Go!" He pushed me away, his voice tight.

I had to obey. I had to leave. To stay with the Bibles would seal our fates.

I could hear voices nearby, the speakers invisible in the dark.

I put my hand out, feeling for the ornamental tree growing in front of my window. I found it and swung my legs over the windowsill.

Dew dampened my feet as I landed in the overgrown grass. I crouched between the house and tree, straining for a glimpse of movement in the back yard. I couldn't see anyone, but the crackle of radios alerted me to police presence.

Staying close to the house, I crept towards the edge of the yard. I prayed the shrubbery would be enough to hide me.

When I reached the woods bordering our property, I stood up. They wouldn't see me in the shadows of the trees, and their brisk chatter hid any sound I might make.

A great crack shattered the night air. They'd broken the door. I didn't look back. Couldn't look back.

Squeezing my eyes shut, I forced myself to concentrate on following my memorized path to the lake.

The ripples on the water glinted in the faint moonlight. I stopped at the bank and squeezed the books in my hands. It felt like holding red-hot coals, yet I dreaded destroying them.

The breeze shifted. It carried the sound of shouting.

I dropped to my knees and scooped dirt and rocks into the plastic bag. When it felt heavy, I added *Do Hard Things*, my Bible, and the new red Bible.

I saved Dad's Bible till last. It weighed heavy in my hands. Almost as heavy as my heart. So many nights I had watched Dad pour over this book. So many mornings I listened to him read it. So many times in my childhood both my parents and I had gathered around its pages seeking comfort and wisdom. I couldn't do it.

Another shout reached me. Dad crying out in pain. I pressed the back of my wrist into my mouth, stifling the sobs that threatened to break loose.

Shadows separated from the house, heading toward the lake. I tied a loose knot in the bag, tight enough to hold the books in, but not tight enough to keep the water out.

The cops stopped halfway between the house and lake. Definitely Agency. The silhouette of their slouched hats confirmed my suspicion.

If they stayed still a moment longer, I could get rid of the Bibles before they came close enough to hear.

Mud squished between my toes as I edged close to the lake. I glanced over my shoulder. The men still stood near the house. I leaned over the water and tossed the bag. It plunked out of sight, sending ripples shimmering across the surface.

Clutching Dad's Bible against my chest, I hunkered behind a tree and watched the police. They were walking again, approaching the lake. Had they heard the splash?

I squeezed the Bible harder. If they caught me, they'd probably kill me anyway. What difference did it make whether I held a Bible or was accused of owning one? Perhaps proof of my guilt would earn me a swift death instead of a drawn out trial I could never win.

If they caught me, a fast death would be a mercy. I shivered at the potential of being dragged to prison. Some Christians were executed with no more thought than euthanizing a stray dog. Other times they tried to force the Christian to recant. Only a handful of people who refused to deny their faith survived to tell. I knew all the stories.

Please, God. Not me. Not now.

I didn't think I would recant. Even in my times of despair, I never questioned the truth of my faith. But no one could be sure of their reaction under such pressure until they faced it. I didn't want to find out.

As the men drew closer I realized they were staring intently at handheld screens. The monitors cast a glow across their faces.

A radio crackled to life on one man's belt. A voice came through in bursts of static. "What do you see?"

"The signal is strong, sir, when it comes at all. It keeps cutting out. The battery in the tracker is dying."

"Impossible."

"Yes, sir, I know. It seems the tracker has been thrown into the lake."

The man on the other end cursed. "Don't waste time, then. I want to get out of here before the neighbors show up to find out what's going on. We've secured the prisoner."

Oh, God, You can't let this happen. Please. Tears dripped off my chin.

The moon silhouetted more men coming out the side door of the house. Two of them marched a third man between them. I watched as they forced Dad into the driveway.

My verse wouldn't come to me. I could think of nothing but the torrent of grief.

Please, God, don't take him too.

Chapter Two

I stayed at the edge of the trees all night, my body curled around Dad's Bible. The scent of mud and rotting leaves dominated my senses. I wanted to cry, but the tears wouldn't come.

Finally, at some point, I drifted into a dozing stupor.

A bone-numbing chill woke me just as the first glow of light appeared on the horizon. I hugged the Bible to my stomach, my forehead touching my knees. Sleep hadn't eased the nauseating ache in my chest. I didn't understand. Why would God let this happen to me again? Hadn't I suffered enough?

"Heather?" The low call of a familiar voice broke through my grief. I straightened, kneeling and searching for the speaker.

"Heather? Where are you?" A young man stood in the yard, his back to me.

I brushed away straggles of damp hair that clung to my face and pushed to my feet. "Over here, Bryce."

He swung around, searching the tree line.

I stepped out of my hiding place.

Bryce jogged toward me. "Thank God you're all right." He put his hands on my shoulders and held me at arm's length. The normally faded freckles on his nose stood out the way they always did when he was upset. "You look terrible."

The quiver started somewhere deep inside me and wobbled out as a sob. I threw myself against him. "They arrested Dad."

"I know." He wrapped me in a brotherly hug that released a floodgate of tears. "That's why I came looking for you."

"You know? How? Did Carmen..."

"Nothing from Carmen. I overheard something about it this morning." He hesitated. "From a different source."

His dad. Most of his off-the-grid information came from eavesdropping on his parents. Keeping his faith secret from the people he loved most was one of Bryce's heaviest burdens, but the information he gleaned was an invaluable asset to the church.

"You found a Bible yesterday," he said. "At the sorting center?"

"It was supposed to be for Ansley." I struggled to curb my tears. "I had to throw it."

The air in front of him clouded as he blew out a long breath. "It was a plant."

My head tingled as the blood drained from my face. I pulled away and looked up at him.

"They don't know who took it." He bounced onto the balls of his feet. "But they followed it here. The man making the arrest knew your Dad."

My mind spun. "What do you mean he knew Dad? Did someone turn us in?"

Another shake of his head. "They followed the Bible here. This other guy knew about your Dad already, so he assumed your Dad was responsible."

"He has an alibi." My mind hurried down well-worn paths. "He was at work all day. He didn't come home until after the sorting center closed."

I hesitated. Dad had said the police singled him out at work. They had asked him questions. My legs wobbled, and I steadied myself against a tree. I couldn't afford hysteria. I needed to think.

"They don't think he took the Bible himself. They just know it led them here." Bryce took my hand and tugged me away from the tree. "You need to get out of here. It's only a matter of time before they realize you volunteer at the sorting center."

Volunteers didn't work set hours and weren't recorded on the list of employees. It gave me a slight safety net, but it wouldn't take long for investigators to trace my student ID.

"Do I have time to pack a few things?" I pulled my hand free of his. Unless the police had found it, my emergency kit would be under my bed. I could add a few clothes and be ready to go.

"I guess so." He glanced over his shoulder.

"I won't take long. Promise." I handed him Dad's Bible and headed for the house.

Bryce hurried to keep up. "You kept a Bible?"

"It's Dad's Bible. I couldn't throw it." I knew Bryce wouldn't agree with my choice. He would have forced himself to throw it, no matter how many memories were linked to it. In many ways, he was braver than me, but living with the governor forced him to be more practical.

"Are you insane?" He tucked the Bible under his arm, but didn't relent from his scolding. "They would have killed you!"

I shrugged. "I don't think it would have mattered."

Bryce stared at me. To him it would have mattered. Dad and I were his family. If the police had found me with the Bible, he would have lost both of us in one day.

"They didn't find me, so it's okay." I wrapped my fingers around the window sill. "Give me a boost?"

Bryce laced his fingers together to make a step for me. I put one foot into his hands. His warm fingers burned against my bare feet.

"Heather, you're freezing."

I threw my free leg over the sill as he lifted me. "Didn't have time to grab shoes."

"Well, grab some now." He let go of my foot and wiped the mud off on his jeans.

"I'll be right back." I slid into my room and almost landed on an overturned nightstand. I took a few cautious steps to the center of the room, careful to avoid the shattered bits of mirror scattered across the floor. Clothing spewed out of open dresser drawers and lay strewn around the room.

I blinked hard. I had cried enough the night before. Tears would change nothing. I needed to get out of here and figure out what to do about Dad.

I bent to retrieve a pair of socks. I couldn't see any glass shards, but I shook them out just to make sure. My black combat boots came next.

With my feet protected from the glass, I sorted through the mess of clothing until I found a pair of black jeans with bell bottoms wide enough to fit around my boots. Finding a shirt was easier. I wore all solids to make matching simple.

Items tucked away in the back of my closet lay in plain sight. So many reminders and memories littered the floor.

I sat down on my bed and pulled a faded sweater to my nose. Mom's scent still clung to the soft fabric. Ever so faint but still there.

"I'm so sorry," I whispered.

Tears blurred my vision again. I need to stay focused. My heart ached as I folded the sweater and placed it on the bed. All my mementos, the tokens that reminded me of my parents and my childhood, would be lost to me the moment I left this house.

I pulled my small, emergency travel bag from under the bed and started adding clothing. Dad needed me. I didn't want to fail him as badly as I had failed Mom.

My small bag didn't hold many clothes, but I didn't need much. I added Mom's sweater on an impulse. I had to leave almost everything behind, but with Dad's Bible and Mom's sweater, I could keep a piece of both of them.

"Heather?" Bryce's tone made me picture him shifting from one foot to the other.

"Almost done!" I needed to get my coat from the living room.

My breath caught in my throat as I left my room. Holes polka-dotted the walls. The framed pictures that once created a family timeline down the length of the hallway now lay shattered on the floor. I stooped to pick one up. The cracked glass revealed a picture of me smiling from between my parents.

I was around four when the picture was taken. We'd taken a day trip to a nearby lake. I could see a faint sunburn on Mom's nose and cheekbones.

I slipped the photo out of the frame and slid it into my bag. The pressure in my chest kept growing.

I hurried through the kitchen, trying to ignore the devastation. It was a good thing I didn't plan to stay here. It would take a long time for one person to reverse the mess.

My leather jacket still hung by the door. I wondered why the cops hadn't thrown it on the floor and trampled it like everything else.

I lifted it off the wooden peg. The familiar scent of leather and books surrounded me as I tossed the coat over my shoulder.

One of Dad's slippers tripped me as I turned to leave. I scanned the room for its companion. Had the police allowed him to stop long enough to put on his shoes?

My quick search didn't reveal the missing slipper. I nudged the stray one into place by the door. I had started putting Dad's slippers by the door when I was little. It was my way of welcoming him home from work. The little routine felt right, but the missing slipper widened the ache in my heart.

I hurried back to my room, illogically afraid of leaving through the same door Dad had.

Where would Dad be now? I doubted they had transported him all the way to the main city last night. I pictured the huge, dark city prison and shuddered. No

Christian wanted to pass through the gate in that tall, electrified fence.

If Dad wasn't at the main prison, he was probably at the local outpost.

I stepped into the bathroom to grab my toothbrush and checked myself in the mirror. Dark circles of mascara ringed my eyes. Dirt smeared my face and stuck to my hair.

I turned on the faucet and scrubbed my face.

"Heather, hurry." Bryce was pacing. I could hear him through the open bathroom window.

"Coming." I checked myself in the mirror again. I looked exhausted but human. A definite improvement. At least I wouldn't draw attention because I looked like a zombie.

I went back to my window and pulled up the blinds.

"You okay?" Bryce tipped his head back to look at me.

"I don't have time not to be." Another one of those neutral answers that masked the true feelings of my heart. Voicing those feelings would venture onto dangerous ground. If I didn't talk about them for long enough, they would grow numb and I could ignore them. It had worked in the past.

Bryce frowned.

"Here, take this and get out of my way so I can jump." I tossed him the bag to prevent him from pressing further.

"Are you sure?" He stumbled back to catch it. "I could help you down."

"I've practiced this more times than I can count. It's easier to jump."

"Okay." He stepped to the side.

I swung my other leg over the sill and launched myself out. My knees absorbed the impact, allowing my body to coil to the ground. The feathery, evergreen branches of the ornamental tree brushed against my face.

"You sure you're okay?" Bryce stepped forward and offered me his hand.

"Fine." I hauled myself up.

"My bike is over by the side of the house." Bryce tucked Dad's Bible into my bag. "I'm going to take you someplace safer."

I glanced back at my bedroom window. I had never known any other home. Everything familiar was in this house. I knew heaven was my only true home, but that consolation felt empty. Heaven didn't have a roof and walls and a lifetime of memories.

Bryce tapped my shoulder. "It's not safe to stay here. It's only a matter of time before they figure out who took that Bible."

"I know." I needed to stop mourning the loss of a building and focus on what to do next.

"I don't fancy being here when the police come back to take over the house. And I really don't want you to be here either."

My throat tightened. All of our pictures. Mama's wedding dress.

"Heather." Bryce grabbed my hand and tugged me away from the window. "We have to go. You knew this could happen."

"Stop it!" I pushed him away. Tears blurred my vision. No, no, no. No tears. Not yet.

"Hey." Bryce wrapped an arm around my shoulders and pulled me into a hug. "I'm sorry. I just want to keep you safe."

"I know." I sniffled and rested my forehead against his chest. If I closed my eyes I could almost imagine he was Dad. Almost, but not quite.

"We really have to go." He pulled away and grabbed my hand again.

I let him pull me along, my mind spinning. "I want to go to the prison."

Bryce froze mid-step.

"The local one. Not the big one." I couldn't get into the big one without authorization or internment orders.

Bryce rotated to face me. "That's not the safe place I had in mind."

"They might have Dad there." I grabbed my bag from him and dug through the mess of clothing. When I found the small zip-lock bag buried at the bottom, I pulled it out. The clear plastic revealed a wad of bills. Our emergency fund. "I might be able to bribe the guards to release him."

"No. Just, no." Bryce shook his head. "I promised your father I'd take care of you if anything ever happened. I can't let you waltz into a prison. That's the number one place we should avoid."

"I could just refuse to go with you." A familiar stubborn feeling rose inside of me. It scared me.

"Don't make this harder than it needs to be."

I jerked my hand away from him. "I can't just forget about Dad."

"I'm not asking you to forget. But there's nothing we can do about it."

I shook my head. "Maybe I can."

"Heather, stop." He reached for my hand, but I put it behind my back.

"I made a promise to your dad," he said.

"This is the first I've heard of it." I could hear the edge in my voice.

"He didn't want to worry you." Bryce grabbed my arm and pulled my hand from behind my back. "Now stop."

My heart pounded. I didn't want to do this. Didn't want to go down this path again. The last time I stubbornly insisted on getting my own way it had developed into a nightmare. I never wanted to repeat that mistake again.

"You don't have to come with me," I said. "I'll go on my own." I had to try to help Dad, but I didn't have to risk Bryce's life in the process.

Bryce's expression softened. "Come on, Heather. I'm not the enemy here. I just can't let you throw your common sense away."

I took a deep breath. No matter how strong my determination, I had a hard time saying no to Bryce.

"I can't let you go to the prison." Bryce used the same soothing voice he would for a small child. "It isn't safe. Your dad is too well known. Someone will recognize you."

"Dad's the public one. I doubt anyone remembers he has a daughter."

Bryce pursed his lips. "The police have been looking at his records, Heather. And they have your student ID from the sorting center. They know about you."

"I'm going to the prison," I said. "You can't change my mind. I'll go by myself."

"Heather..."

"Don't *Heather* me. I've heard of bribes getting Christians out of prison. I have to try."

"Nothing I say is going to change your mind, is it?" His shoulders sagged.

"No." I couldn't stand the thought of losing Dad when there was a chance I could save him. It was a fool's errand, but I had to try.

Bryce sighed. "Let's go. You want to take your bike or ride on mine?"

"I'll take mine and go on my own." I hadn't touched my bike since Mom died. It seemed appropriate to resurrect it now.

"That wasn't an option."

"I don't want you to come with me." I started walking around the house.

"You'll never get air in your tires. They're all cracked." He grabbed my arm and redirected me. "We'll take my bike."

I perched on the passenger pegs attached to the back wheel of Bryce's bike as he peddled through the sleeping neighborhood. Rose-colored rays of sunlight glowed against the houses. I took a deep breath of the crisp, spring air, trying to calm my nerves.

My bag swung from the handlebars. Its zipper clicked against the frame of the bike like a ticking clock.

The wad of bills pressed against my leg. I let go of Bryce's shoulder with one hand to touch my pocket as Dad's voice rang through my memory.

This is in case there's an emergency, Heather. He shifted to hold my gaze when I tried to look away. *If anything ever happens to me, you can use this money to live on.*

If I couldn't bribe the guard, I'd use the money the way Dad meant me to. If I could bribe the guard, we'd figure something out together.

"What are you going to say?" Bryce's voice pulled me out of my thoughts.

"Say?"

"At the prison? To the police?" Sarcasm laced his words.

"Don't be grouchy."

"I'm not."

"You sound it." I knew I should cut him some slack. My behavior had him on edge. I'd probably get myself arrested and not do Dad a speck of good. I just hoped I didn't get Bryce arrested—or worse—in the process.

I forced my mind back to Bryce's question. "I don't know what I'm going to say."

"Wrong answer." The bike swerved as he turned his head to look at me.

"Watch where you're going!" I slapped his shoulder, and he looked back at the road. The bike straightened out, the wheels making a faint humming sound as Bryce peddled.

"It's still the wrong answer," he said after a minute.

"It's a fine answer." I stalled, searching for a verse hovering at the edge of my brain.

"Heather..."

I remembered the verse and cut him off. "Take ye no thought how or what things ye shall answer, or what ye shall say: for the Holy Ghost shall teach you in that same hour what ye ought to say."

"Luke 12:11 and 12," Bryce answered automatically, trained by years of playing our memory game. He hesitated. "I still don't like it."

"Yeah, well, I'm not big on Dad being in jail."

"Neither am I."

"I can't sit back and do nothing." I worked to keep my voice steady. If Bryce realized I might start crying at any moment, he'd never let me follow through.

"I'm not trying to be difficult, Heather. I'm on your side, remember?"

A car passed us, cutting a little too close for comfort. I tightened my grip on Bryce's shoulders and squinted at the still-dim sky.

"Government vehicle," Bryce said. The government could afford batteries to store the solar power.

I rotated my shoulders and relaxed my death grip.

"I hear you on the verse, Heather, but it wouldn't hurt to have something of a plan. You can let God guide you in what to say, but what are you going to do if they know who you are and try to arrest you?"

"Run. If they try to arrest me, I'll run." The men last night had been Agency, and no one tried to resist Agency men. Most if not all of the officers at the local prison would be regular police. I still preferred to avoid them, but they didn't strike fear into my heart the way Agency police did.

"They'll run faster. You know full well how effective running is." We'd both seen people fleeing from the police. Not many succeeded in getting away.

"I can do it. I'm almost positive." I loved to run, and I could beat just about anyone at school if I wanted to. Getting hired as a cop didn't make a cop fast or devoted to his job.

"I know you're fast, but..." Bryce kept worrying. He wouldn't be Bryce if my blustering soothed his concerns.

I tried again. "Bryce, c'mon. If they recognize me, what other choice do I have?"

He fell silent for a moment. "Good point."

"I'll run through the houses and try to lose them. If it works, I'll come back to you, and you can bring me wherever it is you want me to go."

He flashed a smile over his shoulder. "That's the best idea you've come up with yet."

Bryce braked behind the old, brick police building, a relic from before the war. The police used it mostly as a command center, a place for the higher-ups to work and the officers to report. They used the cells to hold temporary prisoners. Even if they planned to send Dad to the big, modern prison in the main city, they'd probably keep him here for a night or two.

I hopped off the passenger pegs and wiped my sweating palms against my pants. My stomach churned.

"You okay?" I could see the concern in Bryce's expression.

Okay? What a joke. "Yeah. Fine. Pray for me?"

"I've been praying."

I could feel myself zoning out on him. All of my concentration focused on the task ahead. I rubbed my hands across my pants again. My brain screamed that I could still back out.

My efforts would probably backfire. I could end up getting myself and Bryce arrested or killed. Maybe both. I felt like puking. *God, what am I doing?*

"Heather?" Bryce waved a hand in front of my face.

I blinked.

"I didn't think so. You didn't hear a word I said." He shook his head and pulled me into a hug. "Be careful."

"Okay." I wiggled free and ran my fingers through my hair. A brush would be better, but it would do. I twisted it into a ponytail. "How do I look?"

"Better." He tucked a loose strand behind my ear. "Less gothic and more tired than usual, but better."

"It'll work."

"Don't do anything stupid." The corners of his eyes tightened the same way they did on the way to our underground meetings. He was tense, but trying to stay calm.

"I'll be right back." I flashed a smile that probably looked as forced as it felt. Too late to back out.

"Be careful."

As careful as Daniel in the lions' den. I didn't say it out loud. Instead, I nodded and jogged around the corner of the building. *God help me.*

Chapter Three

Breathe deep and stay calm. I straightened my shoulders and slowed my pace as I neared the front door of the police station. *Act like you have nothing to hide.*

Easier said than done. After a lifetime of avoiding the police, my instincts screamed at me to run. I concentrated on exuding an aura of confidence.

The front door swung open, and two uniformed men hurried out, consulting a piece of paper.

Keep going. Act natural. Like there was anything natural about this whole situation.

The two police glanced at me, gave me a quick once over, and never broke stride. They jogged down the stairs and kept going.

My heart drummed in my chest. I forced myself to stop watching them. Instead, I stared up the stairs at the door. *Just a building. Just a door. No big deal.* Except it was a big deal. *Get over it.*

I mounted the steps and pulled the tall, glass door open. Stepping inside, I found myself in a huge room with a vaulted ceiling and tiled floor.

For a moment I thought the grand entrance room was abandoned. The sound of the door bumping shut reverberated through the silence.

"Can I help you?" The voice echoed, and it took me a second to locate the speaker. A woman with frizzy bangs and a ponytail sat half-hidden behind a big reception desk.

I reminded myself about exuding confidence and strode over to the desk. The clomp of my boots filled the room.

The woman raised her eyebrows as I stopped in front of her. I placed her in her mid-forties. Around Dad's age. The name plate on the desk read Mirabella Oxford.

"I'm here to ask about a prisoner you may be holding." I leaned my forearms against the counter. *Please, God, let this work.*

Her eyebrows drew together.

"He was arrested last night, I think."

She tapped a screen on her desk, using her index finger to flip virtual pages. "Name?"

"Mine or his?"

Mirabella looked up and frowned her disdain. "The prisoner's."

"Rayford Scott Stone."

If she recognized his name, she didn't let on. She flipped more pages and tapped something into an onscreen keyboard. Another glance. Another frown. She pressed a transmitter clipped to her ear. "Officers

32

Peterson and Girdelli, report to the front desk. Repeat, Peterson and Girdelli to the front."

"Is he here?" I resisted the urge to fidget.

"The officers will be here to assist you momentarily." She continued tapping her screen, not bothering to look up at me.

I tried to quell the rising panic. Why did she need two officers to tell me if Dad was here?

Her hand went back to her ear. "What's that? Oh. Yes, I will."

She released the ear piece. "Peterson and Girdelli are in the process of transferring a prisoner. You may have a seat and wait for their convenience." She pointed to a row of armchairs against the far wall.

I hesitated, a hundred questions jumbling into my mind. Why couldn't she just tell me if Dad was here or not? Should I tell her about the bribe?

Mirabella glared at me, and I resisted the urge to raise my hands in mock surrender. *I'm going. I'm going.*

Bryce would be worried sick when I didn't come back right away. He was probably right to worry. Something was out of place.

I walked to the arm chairs but didn't sit down. I needed to talk to someone about exchanging the cash in my pocket for Dad.

My head throbbed. *Please, Lord, help me.*

I glanced across the room at Mirabella. Only her ponytail showed above the desk as she bent over her work. No change. Everything felt too quiet. Too peaceful. No bustle of people with paperwork. No one walking in and out. No hum of coworkers talking on their way to get a drink or use the bathroom.

It reminded me of the stillness before a big storm.

I needed to get out. Mirabella's screen knew where Dad was. For some reason she didn't want to tell me. I doubted her intentions were in my best interests. And what about those two officers I was supposed to be waiting for? If they were the ones assigned to Dad's case, who were they transporting?

I tiptoed towards the exit. The tiles didn't make any betraying squeaks as inched across them. I opened the door just enough to squeeze through.

The cool morning air enveloped me like a hug, but my breath still felt restricted. I touched the money in my pocket. Where would they take a prisoner to transfer him?

My head buzzed. I forced my lungs to accept a deep breath. After two years of avoiding risks—of avoiding life—I could feel myself coming alive. I had something worth fighting for.

I ducked behind a bush and pulled my boots on. Someone shouted in a side alley, and I heard the rumbling of a large vehicle.

I crept to the edge of the building and peeked around the corner. Sure enough, a boxy armored truck sat in the narrow alley. The agency symbol flashed across the side of the cab, red and silver detailing contrasting with the black of the rest of the vehicle.

The back doors of the truck flung open. They swung back and forth several times before stopping. A cop jumped out of the truck and stood next to it. He wasn't the one I needed to talk to. Peterson and Girdelli would be inside with the prisoner.

A door cut into the brick wall swung open as I watched. Two officers came out, escorting a prisoner between them.

My breath caught in my throat when one cop shifted, and I caught a glimpse of the prisoner. Dad. He didn't hold himself as erect as usual, but the rising sun outlined his tousled hair. He wore one slipper, his other foot bare.

I pulled the money out of my pocket and clenched it in my hand. The limp bills stuck to my moist palms.

My heart pounded as I stepped into the alley.

"Hey! Hey, there!" I jogged towards the police.

Dad's eyes widened when he heard my voice. I could see fear and disbelief flicker across his face as he turned towards me.

The cops turned too, scowling.

"I need to talk to you." Not the most intelligent introduction, but the best my scrambling brain could muster. Confidence. I needed to exude confidence.

"We're busy, kid." One of the cops turned away and pushed Dad towards the car.

"No, please, wait."

The other policeman stared at me, forehead creased. "You look familiar."

"You don't know me." I tightened my fist around the money and resisted the urge to glance at Dad.

"Yeah. Yeah, you've been on the tube."

"Me?" I hadn't made any screen appearances since Mom died. This guy's memory worked way too well.

"You're right." The other guy turned back. "She is familiar." He glanced at Dad, and I could see the connection forming.

"You're right. I've been on the tube." I decided to tell the truth before they figured it out on their own. "I'm Heather Stone."

Dad made a sound somewhere between a gasp and a groan. I ached to go to him.

The cops stared at me.

Yes, I'm just as stupid as I seem to be.

"I'm Heather Stone. I'm here to find out how much you want for his freedom." I pointed to Dad with my free hand.

After a long pause, one of them barked a laugh. "You're crazy."

"What do you mean to imply about us." The other man took a step towards me.

I backed away, watching both of them. "I have money. I'm willing to pay."

"Heather." Dad's voice cracked.

"We don't take bribes. Not for someone like this."

My stomach churned. I needed this to work.

I glanced towards Dad. A dark bruise on his cheekbone stood out against the paleness of his face. He still wore his night clothes.

"What do you want?" I looked back at the cops. "Whatever it is, I'll find it."

The taller one stepped towards me again. "We want our jobs, kid. And we intend to keep them."

His tone of voice didn't give me much room for hope. I didn't understand. Police loved bribes. These men weren't Agency. They didn't have the swagger and brawn that set Agency police apart from the rest. Why would these cops decide to have consciences now?

"You don't even know how much money I have."
I tried again. If I could get them interested it wouldn't
be hard to keep their attention.

"Orders are coming from the top on this guy." The
man jerked a thumb at Dad. "Sorry. But no go."

I backed up. My brain scrambled for an argument
that might make them reconsider.

"We should take you in too." The cop lunged for
me.

I jumped back, jerking my arm away just in time
to keep it out of his grasp.

"Heather, run!" Dad jolted towards us as if trying
to push me away. "You're wanted, ru-"

The cop backhanded Dad across the mouth.

I spun away from another attempt to grab me.
Adrenaline fired though my body. I sprinted away,
trying to block out the image of the policeman hitting
Dad.

Pain jolted through my shoulder. My shoe caught
on the uneven pavement, and I lost traction.

Hours of fall training clicked in as I hit the
ground. I rolled, ready to jump to my feet again. Pain
burned through my side this time.

The cop towered over me, liquid stun gun poised
for another shot. I didn't see the boot heading for my
ribs till it crashed against me. The force shoved my
body sideways several inches.

I bit my lip until I tasted blood. The heels of my
hands throbbed where the cement had peeled the skin
off.

"Up." The guard grabbed my hair and jerked me
to my feet. He glanced over his shoulder. "How much
is your freedom worth to you?"

I opened my clenched fist and stuffed the money into his hand. *Stupid, stupid, stupid.* Now I didn't have Dad or any money to feed myself.

"How much is it?" The guard smoothed the bills.

"Enough," I said. I didn't wait for him to count.

Chapter Four

Bryce stood clutching the handles of his bicycle. He looked like a frightened rabbit, ready to flee at any second.

"Bryce," I almost crashed into him before I caught my balance and skidded to a stop.

"Heather, thank God!" He steadied me. "What happened?"

"We need to get out. They might come after me. Go that way." I pointed in the opposite direction from the alley with the transfer vehicle.

Bryce didn't waste time. He threw his leg over the bike and started peddling before I had both feet on the passenger pegs. I grabbed for his shoulder and pulled my other foot up.

He steered down a side-street directly behind the building, then turned right onto a larger street and picked up speed.

My heart still pounded. I blinked back tears and gritted my teeth. I had failed. Why would a high-ranking person take special interest in Dad? Why did things have to go so drastically wrong again? Why us? How could I be stupid enough to lose another parent over the same thing? I thought I knew what I was doing. I thought I could do it without getting caught.

I squeezed my eyes shut. The flow of thoughts continued to bombard me, rushing through my heart instead of my brain. Too many feelings. Emotion fed illogical actions. I needed to be rational. For once in my life I had to come up with a sensible plan. I had to find a way to help Dad instead of making the situation worse.

How could I do that? Where should I start?

I needed to know the charges against him and find out the date of his trial. I needed to talk to members of the underground.

The thought struck like a punch to the gut. Two years ago I had turned my back on the people in the underground. I lost my passion for the more complicated workings of the network and walked away. How could I go back asking for help after I abandoned them?

"What happened?" Bryce's voice jumped an octave. He cleared his throat. "You were gone forever."

"I had to find the people I needed to talk to."

"Find them?" He glanced over his shoulder. "Why did you need to find them?"

"Watch where you're going!" I slapped his shoulder. "I thought we went over that rule earlier."

He rolled his eyes but faced forward again. "I'm listening."

"The receptionist wouldn't tell me if they had Dad, so I snuck out to talk to the cops." Talking about it brought the impact of my failure into focus. I hadn't saved him. I hadn't even helped him. Now he would face the city prison and its horrors. Alone. Well, not quite alone. *Please, God, be enough for him.*

"You did what?" Bryce's voice cracked again.

"You know you sound like you're thirteen instead of seventeen." I stalled, trying to pull my thoughts together. His voice always went high, like an adolescent boy, when he was indignant or nervous.

He ignored me. "You're a mess. What happened?"

"The receptionist told me to wait for these two officers who were transporting a prisoner. It felt wrong, and what prisoner would they be transporting anyway? So I snuck out and went to find the cops on my own. They had Dad, but they didn't want to hear anything about a bribe."

"And they just let you go?"

"Not exactly. They recognized me. One guy tried to grab me, so I gave him the money. It delayed him long enough for me to get away."

"What happened to your hands?" He sounded like an anxious parent. He must have noticed the scrapes when I first ran up.

"I fell on the sidewalk." My injuries still throbbed. The pain in my shoulder and side overshadowed the ache from the fall. "I went to run and the guy shot me with his stun gun."

"Stun gun?" Bryce yelped. "What do you mean stun gun?"

"Shh!" I reached around and slapped my hand over his mouth. "You know what a stun gun is. I got shot by one."

"Er 'ot 'erious." He mumbled into my hand.

I let go of his mouth. "Assuming you just told me I'm not serious, the answer is, yes. I'm serious. I've got a burn on my shoulder to prove it."

"We need to get you somewhere to clean up." He sounded calmer.

"I need to talk to someone who can find out what's going on with Dad." I doubted anything could be done for my stun gun wounds, and my scraped palms just needed soap, water, and disinfectant. Both injuries could wait.

He sighed. "I'll tell you what. I'm still bringing you to that safe house, but we could swing by Carmen's first if you want."

A smile tugged at my lips. "Yes, please."

We parked the bike in a clump of bushes half a block away from Carmen's house.

"Keep your head down." Bryce slung an arm around my shoulder. "There're some people on the road."

"Got it." I tucked my chin into my jacket and leaned into him. The boyfriend-girlfriend ruse seemed to work well when we wanted people to ignore us. People saw a couple and ignored us as individuals.

I always wondered if the ruse made Bryce feel a little awkward. We treated each other like brother and sister, but Dad suspected it might turn into more someday. Thinking about that made my cheeks warm.

Silly girl. I scolded myself. How could I even think about that at a time like this?

Bryce removed his arm as we slipped into Carmen's back yard. "Sorry about that."

"It's okay." I managed a quick smile, hoping the blush had faded from my face.

Bryce knocked on the back door.

The curtains fluttered. Carmen's face appeared in the window for a second. Her dark, dramatically outlined eyes widened when she saw us. She dropped the curtain.

I felt better just seeing her, but she needed to be more careful with that check out the window.

Seconds later, the door opened. Carmen grabbed my wrist, dragging me inside. "Thank God you're okay. I've been so worried."

Bryce closed the door behind him. "I take it you know something's wrong."

I tipped my head back to catch her reaction.

"Some weird stuff happened last night with Ray's government profile." Carmen hugged me. "I couldn't get a message to you. Not without taking too big of a risk. Is he okay?"

"No." I pulled away and twisted my hands together. "They arrested him last night."

One hand fluttered to her chest. "I'm so sorry. I ... I should have found a way."

"It's not your fault, Carmen." Bryce squeezed her shoulder. "You're in a touchy spot. We can't have you taking risks."

Before becoming a Christian, Carmen had been a poster girl for the government's youth training program. When she got saved, she maintained her government job and continued climbing through the ranks.

I had always admired her. She used her access to government databases to warn us about upcoming arrests or subversive material searches. She knew the identities of more Christians than anyone else. If anyone knew what was going on with Dad, it would be Carmen.

"What happened to you?" She turned my hands palms up and touched the peeled skin.

"Ow! Stop." I jerked them away. "I fell."

"Can you help fix her up?" Bryce asked. Worry-wart.

"I'll do my best." Carmen reached for my wrist again.

"But—"

Bryce cut me off. "Get patched up first. Then we'll talk."

Carmen lifted her eyebrows but didn't ask questions. "Come on. Some of that blood is starting to dry. We'll have to soak it off in the sink."

Carmen performed her first aid efficiently. The peeled skin on my palms stung but didn't amount to much. My shoulder hurt a lot more. We spread ointment over the burn, but most of the damage was inside.

I left Carmen cleaning the bathroom. My limbs felt heavy. Exhaustion swept over me as the adrenaline weakened.

"You okay?" Bryce jumped up from the couch when I entered the living room.

"Yep. Banged up but nothing that won't heal." I pushed him back onto the couch and sat next to him. "Carmen's worrying me. She hasn't mentioned Dad at all since I told her he got arrested."

I couldn't always read Carmen, but I knew she dealt in facts. Her feminine ways often contrasted her blunt way of stating the truth. I liked that about her. It was one of the things that made us get along well even though she was thirteen years older than me.

"I think she's just focused on taking care of you."

"Maybe." I tipped my head back against the couch and closed my eyes. My head throbbed.

Bryce reached over and massaged the back of my neck.

"Oooh." I groaned as his fingers dug in. "That's good. Painful but good."

Carmen walked into the room and sat down across from us. "I'd offer to let you sleep here a while, but you should probably get to that safe house as soon as possible."

"Do you know anything about Dad?" I shrugged Bryce's hand away. "Can you find out what's going on? That's why we came here."

Carmen bit her lip. My heart sank.

"What's that mean?" Bryce asked.

Carmen leaned towards us, folding her arms across her knees. "I'm not quite sure how to explain."

My heart rate sped up.

Bryce squeezed my shoulder. His eyebrows scrunched together.

"Last night I turned on my screen to check on all the members of our gathering. I do it every night before I go to bed. Pull up everyone's profile and make sure no alerts have been posted to them." She hesitated, pushing a strand of hair behind her ear and staring at the carpet. "Ray's file wasn't where it was supposed to be. I searched for hours." She lifted her head and made eye contact. "Heather, according to the government records, your father does not exist."

I froze, trying to decipher what she meant.

Bryce voiced my fear. "You—you mean he—he's dead?"

Carmen shook her head, and I gasped in relief.

"I mean," she said, "that according to the government database, Rayford Scott Stone never existed."

"But what does that mean? Why would they wipe him off the database?"

"I don't know." Carmen shook her head. "I've never seen anything like it, and I can't ask questions."

God, please protect my father. Please, give him strength.

"So there's no way of finding out where he is?" Bryce said.

"No way. Not unless there's information on the higher level databases, but I don't have access to those."

"But I want to do something!" My hands curled into fists.

Carmen leveled a steady gaze at me. "Right now, young lady, the main thing you need to do is keep yourself away from the police."

My cautious instincts agreed with her. I needed to lay low for a while. Christians being arrested put all the rest of the Christians at risk. Dad knew a lot and so did I. If either of us cracked under interrogation, it would be disastrous for a lot of other people.

"You'll let us know if you figure anything out?" Bryce asked.

Carmen nodded. "I'll send a messenger to the safe house."

The safe house. They both kept using the same term, but I couldn't recall ever having a designated safe house. Was it something new in the two years since Mom died? Or were they trying to hide something from me?

"That should work." Bryce got up and shuffled towards the door. "We should keep moving. We're putting Carmen in danger staying here."

"Shouldn't I go on my own then?" I resisted the urge to pull him back onto the couch. "I mean, I'm putting you in danger too."

"Be quiet." He grabbed my hand and pulled me after him. "Your Dad asked me to take care of you, and I intend to do the best I can."

Carmen smiled. "Besides, it's not the first time Bryce has helped us relocate someone."

Bryce grinned at her and tugged me toward the door.

I held back a sigh. I didn't want to leave. Didn't want to go back out that door and face the dangerous world. I wanted to curl up and shut out the world. Anything besides leave. But Bryce kept pulling on my arm.

"Thanks, Carmen. For everything." I glanced over my shoulder and forced a smile.

"I'll be praying for you," she said.

Bryce opened the door, and I had just enough time to nod my thanks before he pulled me outside.

Chapter Five

The streets were still relatively empty as we climbed back onto Bryce's bike. Sunrise had turned into full morning while we were inside. The soft light and whir of bicycle tires created a soothing bubble around us.

It felt like a quiet time to reflect. A memorial.

I pushed the thought away. Memorials were for when people died. Dad wasn't dead. At least I didn't think he was. Not yet.

I shut my eyes and focused on the wind whipping against my face. *Lord, I need help.*

As soon as the thought formed in my mind, I knew the answer. *My grace is sufficient.*

I know, but...

No buts. My grace is sufficient.

I tightened my grip on Bryce's shoulders and focused on regulating my breathing. *I need You.*

You always need me.

Please help Dad. The worry and fear still pinched at the back of my mind, but I tried to tune it out. I wasn't alone. God had a plan. He was bigger than the mess we were in.

I opened my eyes in time to brace myself as Bryce banked into a sharp turn. He pedaled into a narrow street flanked by tall brick houses. We were leaving the good neighborhoods.

As we kept moving, the grass and trees began to disappear. The roofs kept sagging further and further. I recognized the surroundings. Before long the tall, ramshackle buildings would begin to block out the sky.

I knew this place. I knew this route. These streets used to feel like home. Mom and I used to come here together, the two of us riding side by side on our bikes.

"The safe house." I leaned low so Bryce could hear me. "It's Miss Lucy's."

He shrugged and didn't answer. I couldn't blame him. I had stubbornly refused to even talk about Miss Lucy for all this time. Her house was the last place I had been with Mom.

I closed my eyes. Why did everything make me think of Mom? All my efforts to insulate myself from the pain seemed futile. Why would God put me through this nightmare again? Why would he steal Dad from me too?

I forced myself to take a deep breath. The crisp scent of spring filtered through the rotting smell of sewage seeping through the cracked streets.

Miss Lucy's apartment was a logical safe-house for me. I knew her well, and she cared. She wouldn't mind the risk of harboring me. Despite their age gap, she and Mom had been close friends. I had grown up regarding her as a grandmother.

We whizzed by a grimy kid who waved at us. Bryce waved back.

"Who was that?" I twisted to watch the kid. A child that age shouldn't have been out at that hour of the morning, especially not without supervision. But most parents in the slums seemed oblivious to rules like that.

"His name's Alden," Bryce said. "I've talked to him a few times."

I glanced over my shoulder to catch a final glimpse of the boy. He was watching, but he ducked his head when I looked back.

I sighed. I used to recognize dozens of the slum kids and know many by name. Maybe if I'd never left, I would know Alden.

"You'll be safe here for a while." Bryce slowed to avoid a pothole.

"I know the advantages of the slums." The police ignored this place. Crime and poverty ruled, but we Christians found freedom here.

Mom loved it. Before they killed her, I loved it too.

Bryce turned right, into a tiny alley. Silly, bubbly excitement raced through me for a moment, but it didn't last long. I loved Miss Lucy and she loved me, but how could I face her?

We coasted to a stop, and Bryce put his foot down. "This is the end of the line."

As if I didn't know it.

I jumped off and looked around. The buildings on either side seemed to lean towards each other, almost blocking out the sky. They always reminded me of the tenement buildings from my history book, and I wondered if they could be that old.

Bryce scanned up and down the street before taking my bag and grabbing my arm. He led me up a ramp to a pale blue door.

I brushed my fingers over the faded red house number. 73. Perfection and resurrection. A sign of safety for Christians.

Bryce rapped on the door a couple of times, then pulled a key from his pocket. He unlocked the door and hollered a hello.

I followed him down the familiar, narrow hallway. A tingle raced down my spine. I wondered if the prodigal son felt this way when he returned to his father's home.

"Miss Lucinda?" Bryce called.

"Come right on in, child." A rich voice, mellowed with age, answered him. "Did you bring her?"

"Yes, ma'am."

I wondered how news had reached her so quickly. Carmen had seemed to know of our destination as well. Bryce must have contacted a messenger before he came to get me.

We entered a medium-sized living room. I brushed my foot over the worn, dark wooden floorboard. Framed cross-stitched pictures hung on the walls.

Miss Lucinda sat at the far end of the room. Silver-gray hair tumbled around her shoulders as she sat erect in her wheelchair.

My throat went dry. What should I say? What *could* I say? I started to shove my hands into my pockets but stopped myself.

Miss Lucy's face creased into a smile. "Welcome back."

"Thank you." I managed to keep my voice steady. I needed to apologize.

"Come here, child." She beckoned me closer.

I shuffled to her and stopped by her chair.

She took my hand and squeezed it. "I've missed you."

"I missed you too." I put my other hand on top of hers. Her skin felt soft, like an old, worn leather Bible. I stroked my fingers across the back of her hand, across ridges of scar tissue. "I'm sorry I never said goodbye."

"Sit down, honey. That ain't important now."

I lowered myself onto the sagging couch. Nothing had changed. Fabric hearts covered a few new holes, but all the pre-war furniture sat just as it had the last time I was here.

I closed my eyes. Another house filled with ghosts. I remembered Mom sitting on the couch next to me, laughing.

"Stay stuck in memories and you miss out on the life you're living," Miss Lucy said.

Her voice pulled me back to reality. She always seemed able to read my thoughts. I almost wished my long absence had weakened her knack.

"I don't live in memories." My words come out sharper than I intended.

"You ain't living, child. You're wallowing." Miss Lucy stung and soothed with equal skill. Apparently she thought her returning prodigal needed some stinging.

"Glad to see you too," I mumbled.

She chuckled. "I'm glad to see you no matter what."

"Wish it happened under better circumstances, though." Bryce sat down next to me. "Did you hear what happened?"

"Only the basics."

I leaned back. Miss Lucy's apartment served as the hub for the Christian underground. News went to her before traveling to the rest of the network.

"You know Mr. Stone got arrested last night?" Bryce said.

Miss Lucy nodded. "Something about a Bible with a tracking device in it."

"Yeah." Bryce squeezed my shoulder. "One of the Bibles at the sorting center ended up being a plant. The police followed it to their house."

"I escaped through the window and threw the Bibles into our lake," I said.

"All except this one." Bryce reached into my bag and pulled out Dad's Bible. "I nearly had a heart attack when I saw her holding it."

"Ray's Bible." Miss Lucy's eyes softened. She reached for it.

"I couldn't throw it," I said. Mom and Dad used to lie on the living room floor together, the Bible open in front of them as they read.

Bryce scooted forward to sit on the edge of the couch. "They wiped Mr. Stone off the government databases, Miss Lucy. Why would they do that?"

"Back up and explain." Miss Lucy closed the Bible. "I didn't hear that part yet."

"Carmen told us about it." I slid the Bible back into my bag. "She can't find Dad on the database. It's like he never existed."

Miss Lucy shook her head. "Carmen didn't tell you anything else?"

"She said she's never seen anything like it," Bryce said.

"Neither have I." Miss Lucy tapped her fingers against the armrest of her chair. "And I'm not sure how we can find out what's going on. Carmen's my go-to person for stuff like this."

Not the answer I wanted to hear. How could we find answers if we'd already exhausted our highest-level contact?

"Maybe the info erase was a mistake?" Miss Lucy suggested. "Maybe someone tried to put in information and hit the wrong button. Goofed something up."

"I don't think so." Bryce started shaking his head before she finished. "They have safeties in place in case something like that happens. Backups."

"Backups?" I perked up. "Where do they keep the backups?"

"No place we can get to," he said. "I don't think Carmen has clearance either."

Of course. I should have known we wouldn't be that lucky.

"Maybe his information is down temporarily while they make changes?" Miss Lucy suggested.

"Possible." Bryce shrugged. "Not probable. At least not for this length of time."

"Do you know anyone else who might have connections?" My voice cracked. I cleared my throat.

"Surely someone in the underground knows someone who could find out."

"We'll try our best." Miss Lucy patted my leg. "You know that."

"The whole region knows who Dad is," I said. "They'll want to know what's going on."

Dad called himself a television celebrity. I called him a screen entertainer. Both terms referred to his job hosting celebrities and politicians on the regional live cast. The government's move to wipe his information didn't make sense.

"People are going to ask questions," I added.

"Exactly." Bryce kicked at the leg of the coffee table. "No one will believe he never existed."

"They have a reason for it, though. You can count on it." Miss Lucy pressed her fingertips together, resting her index fingers against her lips.

"That's what worries me." I couldn't imagine how they would justify his arrest to the people accustomed to seeing his articles and live appearances on the screen.

"Most people won't have access to the database to see he's been wiped," Miss Lucy said.

"They expect him on live cast, though," I said. "And they can access the information about him on his datasite and the company datasite."

"Is the information still there? Do you know that?" Miss Lucy raised an eyebrow.

I hesitated. Of course I didn't know. How could I know anything for sure right now? The government could wipe the information off any datasite they wanted to.

"I'll check on my screen when I get home," Bryce offered. Having a rich, government official for a father came with perks. I didn't know anyone else who owned a private wall screen with full internet access. Most teens made do with their limited access, hand-held school screens.

Miss Lucy glanced at her watch, another pre-war relic. "After school, young man. You're going to be late."

"Oh no! Totally forgot school." Bryce bounced to his feet. "I'll go right home after class and check the datasites."

"Perfect." Miss Lucy smiled at him.

Bryce scooped my bag off the floor. "I'll put your bag in the guest bedroom, Heather." He paused. "Actually, I think we'll put *you* in the bedroom too. You could use the sleep."

I couldn't argue. The mention of bed made me yawn.

"Go on." Miss Lucy gave me a little push. "We'll talk more when you wake up."

"Okay." I leaned over and kissed her wrinkled cheek before following Bryce.

I woke to aching muscles. A throw blanket covered me. Miss Lucy's handiwork most likely. She could do just about everything despite her wheelchair.

I sat up with a groan and a yawn. I needed to get out more. A few years ago a cold night and busy morning wouldn't have fazed me.

It took mere moments for the details of Dad's arrest to come crashing back. Remembering stole my breath. The blanket crumpled onto my lap. I picked it up and pulled it around my shoulders. The gauze bandage on my injured shoulder stiffened my movements, but the aching burn from the stun gun had subsided.

Even in the hardest of times you can find God's blessings if you open your eyes. I blinked back tears. I had been around eight years old the first time Dad said that to me.

Out of habit, I started coming up with blessings. I had been able to runaway when the cop shot me with his electrically charged water gun. Dad was still alive. Even if they killed him, I knew he would go to heaven. I had a brother-friend in Bryce and a grandma-ally in Miss Lucy.

I dashed away a tear that trickled down my cheek and reached for my bag. Wiggling my hand through the clothes, I found my handmade journal.

I caressed it, then frowned when I felt something smooth on the back cover. I flipped it over and discovered the photo I'd tucked into the bag. Mom and Dad smiled at me, their joy frozen in time.

God, why couldn't we have stayed like that? I stuffed the picture into the pages of my journal as my tears overflowed. Again. How much could one person cry in one day?

I wiped my face and opened the journal to an empty page.

In my best decorative cursive, I wrote the title to a new poem. *Raining Heart.* An apt description for myself right now.

The words flowed as fast as I could write them. The rhymes fell into place. The rhythm worked.

I never showed my poetry to kids at school. Everyone would laugh at the poems, even if the Christian aspects could be overlooked. Strict, structured, rhyming poetry was a thing of the past. If anyone wrote or read poetry at all, it was dark, mumbo jumbo that didn't follow any rules at all.

In a sense, my poetry was a way of rebelling against the free-for-all way my peers acted. The very format of my poems clung to a way of life obliterated by the new regime. Sometimes I broke off into freer forms, but today I need an old-fashioned sense of safety.

They've taken him away,
And I must not follow.
This is my place to stay,
Despite the sorrow.

Oh, Lord, please take my hand,
And calm my raining heart.
Please help me firmly stand,
And play my part.

We know Your word is truth,
Though others call us fools.
Oh may my life be proof,
That Jesus rules.

Lord, I will speak your word,
No matter what the cost.
Please let your voice be heard,

Counted Worthy

By these the lost.

Counted worthy we rejoice,
For death is not the end,
To follow is my choice,
My life to spend.

I sat staring at the page after writing the last line. *To follow is my choice, my life to spend.* Brave words. I hoped they were true.

I swung out of bed and folded the throw blanket. A digital clock sat on the nightstand. The numbers blinked the time. 2:13.

I couldn't hear movement in the rest of the house.

I crossed the room and stepped into the hall. The door across from mine stood open. Miss Lucy sat with her back to me, an easel in front of her. I padded to her doorway to get a better look.

Her skilled brush strokes depicted towering mountains with a field of tall, purple flowers in the foreground. The flowers bent from an invisible wind.

"Sleep well?" Miss Lucy set her paintbrush down and rotated her chair to face me.

"Like a rock." I didn't know if passing out from sheer exhaustion counted as sleeping well, but I definitely slept soundly.

"You looked like you needed it."

"I did." I nodded at the painting. "It's beautiful."

"My mountains. They make me feel closer to God." She picked at a fleck of paint on her finger, smiling. "I will lift up mine eyes unto the hills, from whence cometh my help."

"Psalm 121:1." I returned her smile. Miss Lucy had taught me the Bible memory game when I was little.

Miss Lucy nodded at the painting. "This one is from the Rocky Mountains. I visited them when I was a little girl. Before the war."

"My mom went there," I said quietly. "When she was little. She loved it."

"My painting can't do it justice." Miss Lucy retrieved her brush. "Why don't you sit on my bed? We can talk while I work."

Her bed sat much closer to the floor than the one in the other room. Miss Lucy needed everything to be low so she could manage from her wheelchair. I remembered Dad and Bryce working together to modify the bed so she could get in and out of it on her own.

I sat down, folding my legs and leaning my elbows against my knees. "Bryce still comes here a lot?"

"Most days before school."

That meant he had to bike all the way from the border of the main city and back by seven o'clock. Talk about dedication.

"He's a good boy," Miss Lucy said. "I don't know what I'd do without him."

"You're not the only one."

Dad loved teaching Bryce how to do odd jobs around the house and Bryce loved learning. They both used their skills to help members of the Church who were too old or frail or disabled to do the jobs on their own.

Miss Lucy shaded a patch of ground beneath a slender tree. "Your father trained him well."

"When did you meet Dad?" I picked a little ball of lint off her blanket.

"During the war." She dabbed more paint onto her brush. "We lived next to each other."

"You and Dad were neighbors in the ghetto?" I had always assumed Dad met her through Mom.

Miss Lucy nodded.

Dad didn't like to talk about the war. He avoided the subject the same way I avoided talking about Mom.

My whole life I'd followed an unwritten rule not to ask questions. If my parents were willing to tell me about their past, they told me. They harbored too many secrets for me to pry.

Now I needed to know. I wanted every scrap of information. Maybe something from the past would provide a clue to the mysterious events surrounding his arrest. "How old were you guys?"

"I believe your father was thirteen when we were in the ghetto. I was thirty-three."

"How did you get to know each other well?" Thirteen and thirty-three didn't seem like normal "best buddy" ages.

"My mother and I helped him after his mother died."

"His mother died in the ghetto?"

Miss Lucy set her paintbrush down and turned to look at me. "You didn't know that?"

I shook my head.

"Poor Ray." She sighed. "Still hasn't gotten over it after all these years."

I leaned forward, the hundreds of questions I couldn't ask Dad rushing into my mind. "How did you get out of the ghetto?"

I had always wondered. According to our history class, most rebel families either signed a pledge of loyalty to the government or were killed. I couldn't imagine Dad signing the pledge.

"We both got out before the war ended." She folded her hands in her lap. "When we first arrived in the ghettos, the war was going well for us. Our hopes were high."

I frowned. "What does that have to do with getting out of the ghetto?"

"Patience, dear." She silenced me with a wave of her hand. "We wouldn't let the guards dissuade us from holding church services. There weren't any men, so the women led at first. As the boys became teenagers, they took over. Quite a few guards came to know the Lord."

She stared at the wall, eyes unfocused, as if she were looking back through the years, and seeing the ghetto services and the guards who became brothers.

"The guards helped you to escape?" I prompted.

She nodded. "We had a system for getting people out. The guards worked with underground organizations to secure forged IDs and find places to stay. Once they had both for a particular person or family, they'd smuggle us out."

"And the other guards didn't notice when people went missing?"

"Sometimes." Miss Lucy went back to her painting. "When they did, the person's neighbors suffered for it. Usually the good guards registered the missing people as deceased or found volunteers to take their place."

"Volunteers?" I couldn't imagine anyone volunteering to take someone's place in a death trap.

"Sometimes they could get political dissenters already in prison to agree to do it. Don't ask me how they got them out of prison to bring them to the ghetto. We didn't ask questions." She shrugged. "Other times men on the outside would volunteer to come in so the women and kids could leave."

"That's amazing."

Miss Lucy nodded. "Another reason you never heard about it from your father. He got out on a fluke. A younger boy was supposed to leave with his mother, but the boy died. Ray looked a bit like the boy, so they sent him instead. He felt guilty about it."

I nodded.

Miss Lucy started adding more flowers to the field. I watched her, letting the silence stretch as I thought about what she'd told me.

After a while I said, "What do I do now?"

"What do you mean?" She dabbed at the painting a few more times, then put the brush down and wiped her hands on a paint-specked towel.

"I mean, what now? What am I supposed to do?"

Miss Lucy rotated her chair towards me and tilted her head. Her hair swung away from her face.

"I don't know what to do. I don't want to just let them take Dad without a fight."

"I thought you preferred not to take risks these days," she said. "Fighting back is risky."

I resisted the urge to kick something. "Obviously the careful route didn't work."

"Your father never tried the careful route."

"Yeah, but all this happened because of me. Not him. The Agency planted a tracking device in a Bible *I* took home from the sorting center."

She nodded. "Bryce told me."

"Why didn't Dad try to do anything when they killed Mom?" My brain detoured too fast for me to rein it in. "People listen to him."

"It was too late."

"Too late for Mom. But maybe it would have changed things somehow. Maybe people would know about the Agency."

"Everyone knows the Agency exists."

"Sure. They know it exists, but they only hear the government's sanitized version of everything." I grunted in frustration. The ignorance of the general population had irritated me for as long as I could remember.

A smile tugged at Miss Lucy's mouth.

"You think I sound silly?"

"No. I think you sound passionate. You sound like your parents."

Tears sprang to my eyes. I lowered my head, trying to hold them back and failing.

"Crying ain't nothing to be ashamed of."

"I'm not ashamed." I brushed my cheeks and looked up. "I'm just tired of crying. Do you think I can find a way to help him?"

Miss Lucy studied me.

"What?"

"That's a dangerous road to travel. Even in your own mind."

"So?" I didn't care if it was dangerous. I almost hoped it was. "Why hasn't anyone tried to stop them, before? Plenty of Christians are braver than me."

"A few have tried," she said. "Not in the past few years, but before that. People weren't ready to listen."

I put my hands behind me and leaned back, keeping my arms straight. "Do you think they're ready now?"

Miss Lucy studied me again, as if trying to make up her mind about something. "Why are you asking that?"

Wasn't it obvious? "I'm tired of being careful."

"Why?"

I stared at her. Was she really that dense?

"Heather." She wheeled up to the end of the bed and put her hands on my knees. "Before you start a war, you have to know what you're fighting for."

I frowned, replaying the words in my head. I knew what I was fighting for. Didn't I? I wanted to explain it to her, but I couldn't find the right words among the jumble of emotions.

Miss Lucy patted my leg. "I'm not trying to dissuade you, child. I like risky ideas. But if you're going to do something like that, you need to know without question that it's the right thing to do."

I nodded even though the words chaffed. Miss Lucy knew things from experience. Her counsel was respected by everyone involved in the underground network. Unfortunately, wise counsel was not always welcomed advice.

"It's kind of like painting." She pointed at her canvas. "You gotta let the paint dry before you let it out into the world."

Chapter Six

I woke to the sound of murmuring voices. I had no memory of falling asleep. A small lamp glowed on Miss Lucy's painting of the mountains. The still-wet purples and greens shimmered like liquid jewels.

My muscles protested as I stretched my arms above my head. Better get over it. If my instincts could be trusted, things wouldn't get easier any time soon.

One of the voices in the other room rose a little. Bryce.

What time was it anyway?

I swung out of bed and stretched again. The clock on the wall read ten after six. When did I fall asleep? Why didn't they wake me up?

Miss Lucy and Bryce looked up when I shuffled into the living room.

"Sleep well, dear?" Miss Lucy patted the couch.

"I slept fine. You should have told me to get up, though."

"You needed to rest."

"Not that much I didn't."

Bryce smirked.

"You shut up," I said, even though he hadn't spoken. I was glad I'd taken the time to pull my hair into a pony tail. It made me look less like a zombie. "What're you two talking about?"

"Your need for sleep." Bryce knew how to be serious, but he loved to tease.

"Before that."

They glanced at each other, hesitating. Those expressions. I didn't want to ask what they meant.

"You checked your screen." I looked at him.

"Your Dad's datasite is 'temporarily unavailable,'" Bryce said. "His profile on the company datasite says it's been removed for police investigation."

So Dad was off all the databases, not just the government ones. His database disappearance wasn't a fluke. I rubbed the back of my neck, trying to ease a growing headache. We were back to square one.

"People are already talking," Bryce said. "Everyone missed his live cast appearance this morning."

I wondered if the attention was a good thing or a bad thing. It seemed government manipulated, so probably a bad thing.

"Did you find any clues about why they would wipe Dad?" I needed something to work off of. Even a little clue would give me a starting point.

Bryce shook his head. "No, but there's something you should know."

"What's that?"

He hesitated, not making eye contact.

"What's wrong? What aren't you telling me?" I tilted my head, trying to draw his attention.

"I'm working on it." He looked up. "I'm just trying to figure out how to say it."

"Straight out usually works best," Miss Lucy said. That philosophy explained a lot about her. You never had to worry about Miss Lucy skirting around her main point.

"It's about my dad." Bryce shifted again, the way he always did when he would rather be doing something—anything—else.

His parents were another topic shrouded by an unwritten rule of silence. They were the proverbial elephants in the room. His father, governor of the north eastern region of the United Fascist States, was well known for hating Christians.

"What about your dad?" I kept my tone neutral. I didn't want to make this harder than necessary for him.

Bryce tucked his chin and stared at the floor. "He was there last night, Heather."

"There? What do you mean?" His dad must have attended the arrest. What else could he mean? But why would the governor accompany the police for something like that?

"You know he has a thing about Christians," Bryce said.

I nodded. Of course I knew. Every Christian in the region knew. Being friends with Bryce made me doubly aware of it.

"He goes to arrests sometimes. Guess he's had an eye on your dad for a while. I heard him tell Mom this morning."

Miss Lucy leaned forward in her chair. "He's been monitoring Ray?"

"On his own, I guess." Bryce shrugged. "That's what he said."

"Interesting," she said. "Very interesting."

"Why is it interesting?" I swallowed past a lump in my throat. The whole thing was awful, but her curious attitude confused me. "I mean, what does it matter now? Dad's already arrested."

"Could be a clue, child."

"A clue?" The man hated Christians. We already knew that.

"Mmmm." Miss Lucy glanced from me to Bryce and back again. "I know something you children don't."

I leaned forward. Miss Lucy always seemed to have extra information, and it was almost always useful. "Are you going to tell us?"

She hesitated, letting silence hang in the air.

"Now's not the time for secrets." I didn't have much right to make demands, but I needed to know. "The more brains working on this, the better chance we have at figuring it out."

No one pointed out that we probably couldn't do anything no matter what we figured out. As long as the people didn't care what was happening, the government could get away with anything.

Miss Lucy seemed to come to a decision. She straightened and looked at us. "Your two fathers knew each other before the war." Her gaze shifted to Bryce. "They were good friends when they were young. Best friends."

My Dad and Bryce's Dad? I looked at Bryce and saw my surprise mirrored on his face.

"You sure you have the right two dads?" I asked.

"My dad was friends with Mr. Stone?" Bryce's voice squeaked.

Miss Lucy chuckled. "Don't look at me that way. I haven't lost my mind."

"Actions speak louder than words." Bryce grunted.

"Your grandfathers—their fathers—fought on opposite sides of the war. Ray and Governor Williams both supported their own fathers and couldn't remain friends. They lost contact during the war. Ray didn't know that Governor Williams knew that he was alive." Miss Lucy frowned the same way Mom used to when she was thinking. I tried to ignore the stab of pain from the thought. "I'd like to know how Governor Williams knew to watch Ray."

"If they were friends before, wouldn't he recognize Dad?" I asked.

"That was a long, long time ago," Miss Lucy said. "Your father changed his name, his whole identity, when he escaped the ghetto."

Every new piece of information she revealed sent my mind spinning. I wasn't the only one haunted by ghosts of the past. It seemed one of Dad's ghosts was very much alive.

"This is giving me a headache." I rubbed my temples. "Actually, the whole thing is a headache."

Bryce snorted his signature snicker. "You got that right."

"It's not funny."

"No." His smile faded. "It's not funny at all."

"What do you think your dad could want with him?"

"Who knows?" Bryce shrugged. "His being a Christian is all the excuse Dad needs for anything."

"But if he knew Dad was a Christian, why didn't he arrest him before?"

"Maybe he didn't have any proof."

"Then why did he start paying attention to Ray in the first place? What made him suspicious?" Miss Lucy pushed her hair back, her lips pursed.

There were any number of ways suspicion could have fallen on Dad. Over the years people we knew had been arrested. We attended regular church services that could be detected at any time. Plus Dad still participated in underground activities I never wanted to hear about.

"Maybe Dad thought he recognized your dad on the live cast but wasn't sure." Bryce stood up and paced to the window. He brushed the curtain back an inch and looked out. "Maybe the Bible being traced to your house was the proof he'd been waiting for."

Miss Lucy pointed at Bryce like Dad did when he selected someone from the audience. "That, young man, sounds likes a logical option."

I nodded in agreement even though neither of them was looking at me. "What does that mean for us?"

"What do you mean, darling?" The wheels on Miss Lucy's chair squeaked as she rotated.

"We're trying to figure out how to do something, right? How does this theory help us?"

"Patience, child."

"We don't have extra time." Patience had never been my strongest virtue.

I looked at her wheelchair and winced. Her paralysis was just part of the price she'd paid for her faith. The government had imprisoned her for trying to share the truth. They had tortured her in an effort to get her to renounce her faith and tell them who she had been working with.

Miss Lucy never told them and never recanted. For some reason, they didn't kill her. But she had been paralyzed.

What if we didn't get to Dad in time? What if they paralyzed him too? Paralysis would be better than death, but I didn't want either to happen.

"I still don't understand why they wiped him off the databases," I said. Wiping people away as if they never existed wasn't normal. It stuck out just like the red Bible. Strange and dangerous.

Bryce turned away from the window and walked back to us. "Whatever the reason, they have the upper hand, that's for sure."

"Who knows what they'll tell the public when questions start in earnest," Miss Lucy said.

The government controlled all dissemination of news. Even if we figured out what was going on, everyone else would believe whatever the government said.

No one wanted to upset the delicate balance enjoyed between our rulers and the people. Our country retained the title of The United Fascist States, but we didn't operate as a Fascist society. In the years after the Second American Civil War—the Great War—the militant society had slipped into a sort of free-for-all lifestyle. No one wanted to return to the way things used to be right after the Christian faction surrendered.

"We need to get to them first," I said.

Their attention turned back to me.

Bryce crossed his arms across the back of the couch and leaned over me. "We need to get what to who before who?"

I took a deep breath and tried to collect my thoughts. "We need to get our side of the story to the general population before the government starts explaining it away like there's not a problem."

"How would we do that?" His forehead wrinkled. "And how is it going to make a difference?"

"Think about it." I stood up and started pacing. "People usually give more consideration to the first opinion they hear about something, right?"

"Um." He hesitated. His mouth quirked. "I guess so."

I could tell my train of thinking made more sense to Miss Lucy, so I focused on her. "Even if we can't figure out the government's intentions in wiping him off the database and datasites, we can at least tell our side of the story before the government propaganda starts. If we can make people *care*, they might do something."

"It's a thought, child," Miss Lucy said. "Best be praying about it before you do anything."

"I'll pray." I fidgeted, scooting to the edge of the couch. "But I think we should make plans now. In case God says yes."

"Would give her something to do in any case," Bryce said.

"Are you talking about me?" I tipped my head back to look at him and raised an eyebrow.

He nodded. "Sure. I mean, putting something together would be a good thing for you to do since you can't exactly go out right now."

"Who says I can't go out?" Here we went again. I had to admit the prison trip hadn't work out as well as I had hoped, but no serious harm done. "Are you forgetting that you've been trying to coax me out of my cautious funk for the past two years?"

"You're totally picking the wrong time to come out of it," he said.

"Beggars can't be choosers."

"Children!" Miss Lucy held up her hands like a referee in one of the many sports games Bryce played. "Now is not the time for arguments."

Easy for her to say. She didn't have Bryce breathing down her neck. I hushed like a good girl, though, and looked at her. Knowing Miss Lucy, she'd have more to say. She did.

"Working on putting something together would keep you busy here and relatively safe." She waggled a finger at Bryce. "And she's right, Bryce." Her eyes twinkled. "Beggars can't be choosers."

"I never begged," he grumbled.

How conveniently he forgot his frustration and concern over the past few years.

"Miss Lucy?" I took a deep breath, thinking hard about my next words. "You don't ... I mean, do you by any chance still have Mom's printing press?"

There. After all this time, the sealed of door was unlocked. Did I dare put my hand on the knob? What kind of memories would tumble out?

"Ah..." A smile creased Miss Lucy's face. "You know, child, I believe I do."

Chapter Seven

We agreed to wait till morning to unearth Mom's old printing press, but when morning came, none of us were thinking about the press.

Bryce's pocket screen sat on Miss Lucy's table. Dad's picture and the headline "Where Did He Go?" filled the display.

"The government already cleared that datasite, but I got the page downloaded first." Bryce leaned on the table, elbows locked, until it tipped towards him. No one scolded him.

"We knew it wouldn't take long for the rumors to start," I said. The government knew the same thing. If they thought they could contain speculation by erasing Dad off the datasites, they overestimated their powers. People's curiosity couldn't be controlled so easily.

"There's more." Bryce pulled a folded sheet of paper from his pocket.

A private pocket screen with extra doo-dads *and* something on paper. It never ceased to amaze me what the wealthy members of society could obtain.

Bryce unfolded the paper and smoothed it out on the table. My face looked back at us from the paper. The headline read, "Still At Large." The paper went on to explain that the daughter of convicted criminal Rayford Scott Stone was suspected to share her father's religion and had yet to be apprehended.

I scowled at the poster. Christianity wasn't like rabies, and getting Christian's off the streets wasn't as simple as everyone seemed to think.

"Where did you get this?" Miss Lucy wheeled closer to the table to study the poster.

"My Dad's desk. He has a whole stack of them. Hopefully he doesn't count them and realize I've had my hand in the cookie jar."

"They're going to put up paper posters of me? Like in the old days?" I thought of the pictures of paper posters tacked to old telephone poles. The stuff of history.

"Apparently." Bryce spread his hands. "Has me stumped."

"It will grab people's attention, that's for sure," Miss Lucy said.

"It makes Heather sound dangerous." Bryce's lips flattened into a thin line. Protective as ever. I almost hugged him. Almost. I didn't want him to think I appreciated it too much.

"If they make people think she's dangerous, they'll be relieved if she gets arrested," Miss Lucy said. "If they're relieved, they won't ask questions."

"Well, if they're going to make everyone think I'm a threat, I might as well live up to expectations." It made sense. Sort of.

"Making the government feel threatened is a good way to get yourself killed," Miss Lucy said.

I shrugged. "If they're printing these things," I poked at the paper, "they already plan to treat me like a threat. What do I have to lose?"

"She has a point." Bryce scratched the back of his neck.

I grinned at him. Winning him to my side was a good start.

"Maybe you don't have anything to lose, Heather." Miss Lucy picked up the poster and scanned it before looking back at me. "But whatever you do will affect others. People who have plenty to lose."

True enough. But not doing anything didn't guarantee their safety either. Christians quietly disappeared far too often. The government found ways to soothe people's consciences and nothing ever happened. Something needed to change.

"So," I said, "I need to do something that's all on me."

"You against the world?" Bryce shook his head. "I don't like it."

I rested my forehead against the palm of my hand. What would Mom do? When we did things together, she always seemed to know what God wanted from her. I wished I could find the same confidence.

The thought of putting other Christians in danger terrified me. I'd done that once before and it hadn't ended well. At Mom's funeral, I'd promised myself I'd never put myself in a similar situation. Now the similar situation was finding me.

God, what do I do?

If I did nothing, the government's plan for Dad would continue unchecked. It wouldn't end well. Someone needed to start pricking people's dead consciences. The world needed to realize government executions of "undesirable" people wasn't as benign as they seemed to think.

Maybe I could find a way to help Dad and start the ball of change rolling at the same time.

"I think we need to uncover the old printing press," I said. "We can at least start there."

"I don't even know where the secret entrance is." Bryce followed me and Miss Lucy into the living room.

"Can't tell what you don't know," I said. Bryce didn't need the reminder. I figured the sentence had been the mantra of every underground group since the beginning of history.

"It's time for you to find out," Miss Lucy said.

Before I was born, Christians had dug a secret basement for Miss Lucy. Mom and I had spent hours in the secret room, huddled around the old fashioned printing press Dad had crafted from pictures in history books.

Bryce followed us as I pushed Miss Lucy into the living room. Being back in her apartment, leaning on the handles of her wheelchair, felt so natural. I never realized how much I missed her. I had just lumped that loneliness together with my grief for Mom and never recognized it as something separate.

I scanned the wood-paneled wall behind Miss Lucy's couch. As far as I knew, police had never searched her apartment. That alone proved the benefits of living in the slums—and the fact that miracles still happened.

"Did you change the picture?" The cross-stitched picture that hid the tell-tale knot in the wood was missing.

"I surely did." She pointed to a forest scene with spotted fawns peeking between the trees. The threads of the new cross-stitch were vibrant where the last picture had become faded. "It's that one now."

"Gotcha." I lifted the frame off the wall and passed it to Bryce. The knot in the wood seemed normal if you didn't know what to look for. The notch in one side could have been made by a careless workman when the wall was first built. Maybe it was and they converted it later.

I slipped my finger into the cutout and pressed the spring to unlock the hidden door. The latch clicked, and I slid the door back.

"Whoa. Cool!" Bryce tossed the fawns onto the couch and poked his head through the doorway. "It's dark."

"Brilliant deduction." I smirked. "I'll go turn the light on. You'll have to carry Miss Lucy if she wants to come with us."

"You coming?" He turned to her.

"I think so," she said. "Just wait till she gets the light on."

"Twelve stairs down and two steps to the right." I started down the steps.

"You've grown. Your legs are longer," she called after me.

Good point. I hadn't grown much, but the extra inch and a half might change my calculations some. One long stride instead of my old two should work.

I smiled to myself as the pull-string tickled my palm. Right on the money even after all this time. Light from the bare bulb flooded the basement as I tugged the string.

"That's better," Bryce said from the top of the stairs.

I scanned the small room as he clomped his way down. Nothing had changed. Old gray shelves lined two walls. Our work table remained wedged into the corner just where we had left it. My disguise wig perched atop its battered, Styrofoam mannequin head. Only the dust on the table and cobwebs in the corner marked the passage of time. I wondered if anyone had been down here since Mom and I closed the door behind us two and a half years ago.

"Flash to the past, ain't it?" Miss Lucy spoke quietly behind me.

I nodded. I didn't trust myself to speak.

"Press is over there." She pointed to the corner. I'd been avoiding looking. I knew where the press was, but there were too many memories wrapped up in it. Most of them were good, but the last horrible memory tainted them all.

Miss Lucy pointed again. I rotated, moving like a door with hinges tightened by rust. Like everything else, our press looked exactly the way it had last time I saw it. The canvas cloth we used to protect it draped over the top.

I closed my eyes and imagined Mom tossing the cover over the press and patting it like a dog. She loved the machine so much it sometimes felt like part of the family.

I crossed the room and gripped the canvas. Dust coated my fingers, filling the ridges on my fingertips and making them feel smooth.

The memories kept coming. Mom chuckling over the squeak of the press. Mom peeling a page off the wooden type. Mom carefully hand-sewing the binding of a Bible.

A cloud of dust billowed into the air as I yanked the canvas back. Dust motes swirled in the light of the bare bulb.

Bryce coughed and waved his hand in front of his face. "Real smooth, Heather."

"Stop whining." Emotions thickened my voice.

Bryce didn't catch on. "Whining? I'm not..."

"Bryce." Miss Lucy shook her head at him.

I leaned over the press and checked the type. Reading the mirror image letters came naturally. The last chapter of Revelation was neatly laid out, waiting to be inked up.

"Nobody's touched this since Mom died, have they?" I straightened and turned to Miss Lucy.

"I don't think so." She shook her head. "A few people have come down here without me, but I don't think anyone touched it."

I ran my fingers over the type. Dried ink flaked away from the wooden letters. It stained my fingertips.

I put my hand to my nose and took a deep breath of the familiar smell.

"So..." Bryce set Miss Lucy down in a chair. "That press prints actual ink on actual paper?"

"Yep." I held up my stained fingers. "Real ink. Real paper. Real words."

We had everything we needed. Boxes on the gray shelves held our supplies: the paper, ink, type, and binding materials.

"They're real words even on a screen," Bryce said.

"Sort of." The words were real enough. I guessed. But not the same. With the government's access to every connected screen in the country, those words were hard to trust. It was too easy for the government to change them and twist the meaning. Words on paper could be destroyed, but not changed.

"What do you mean 'sort of'?"

"Think about it, Bryce," I said. "What does the government do to words on the screen if it doesn't agree with them?"

"Changes them."

"Words on the screen lie no matter who originally wrote them. Words on paper only lie if the person who wrote them did."

"Okay. I see your point." He swung his hand towards the press. "So what does all that have to do with this?"

I glanced at Miss Lucy.

"Spit it out, child," she said.

"We can do what I mentioned last night. We can print posters that tell the truth and distribute them before Bryce's dad starts handing out his."

"An eye for an eye and a tooth for a tooth?" Miss Lucy raised an eyebrow. The dust floating through the light created a halo around her.

"Not quite." I tried to look more confident than I felt. "Just a paper for a paper."

"The pen is stronger than the sword." She looked past me to the printer. "I suppose your mother would approve."

Would she? I turned it over in my mind. I often made choices based off Mom's imagined advice. This plan...

"It's got her fingerprints all over it," Miss Lucy added.

I turned to study the press and remembered again the affectionate way Mom treated it. She knew the power held by the machine. Power to shape lives and carry fate. Her own death had been linked to it, and she probably found that appropriate.

Me? I wanted to avoid everything linked to her death. But maybe this time the tides would turn. Maybe this time the press could bring life to my family. Maybe pump some life back into our country.

If I failed, I'd suffer a fate like Miss Lucy's. If no one listened, the government would arrest me, assure everyone else that nothing was wrong, and life would continue as usual.

But if I succeeded, people would realize that arresting Dad for being a Christian wasn't okay. Maybe the tables would turn and the government would have to back down. Would they do it? Would the officials sacrifice some of their control in order to keep the peace? Was it possible for a home-produced poster to inspire the people to push the government that hard?

My fingers tingled. It was a far-fetched plan. A fool's hope. But it was Dad's only chance.

Chapter Eight

When Bryce left for school, I settled into my chair at the kitchen table and began drafting ideas for our flyer.

I chewed on the end of my pen. Some character in a book I read as a kid chewed on her pen, and I liked the book well enough to mimic her. Years later I still couldn't kick the habit.

Right now the cracking end of my pen was the least of my worries. It wasn't fair to drag Bryce and Miss Lucy into this whole mess. They had enough troubles of their own without getting pulled into mine.

I put my pen down and rested my forehead on the table. Me and my crazy, stupid ideas. Miss Lucy said Mom would like it, but, after some persuading, Mom had supported the one that got her killed. Not the greatest credentials.

"Writer's block?"

I jumped when Miss Lucy spoke right behind me. Traitorous wheelchair. The thing usually squeaked.

"Kind of," I said.

"Speak what's on your heart, child." She pointed at the piece of paper. "Try plain ol' honesty instead of the manipulation game the government likes."

I doubted my persuasive writing teacher would agree with that perspective. But my persuasive writing teacher worked for the government and groomed young people to do the same.

"I'll try." So now I needed to figure out what was on my heart. Or maybe I shouldn't think too much. Since Mom died, I'd mentally catalogued the injustices countless times. Each day I carried on a silent monologue about the pain caused by persecution. This was my chance to share those thoughts with the world. I lowered my pen to the paper.

My name is Heather Stone. I'm sixteen years old, and I am wanted.

I smirked to myself. If we beat the government to distributing posters, we'd punch the wind right out of their "wanted" announcement. It might even plant a seed of skepticism for whatever propaganda the government rolled out.

Using the printing press revived even more old memories. I found myself reliving things I thought were forgotten. Things I wanted to stay forgotten. I squashed the replays down as much as I could, but some of them refused to be squashed. Thankfully, most of the stubborn memories were good ones.

I sat in the basement cleaning rust off the metal components of the press and reliving hopes and crazy dreams. Mom and I were both dreamers. Together we thought we could change the world. Throw Dad into the mix, and we had no question about it.

Most of the dreams turned to dust after Mom's funeral. Maybe she was the real dreamer. Cleaning the press reminded me of my determination. The problems we had wanted to conquer and mountains we wanted to climb were still there.

Somewhere in my desperation to not make the same mistakes again, I had let go of all the things Mom hoped I would do. She taught me to print Bibles because she wanted me to continue her work after she died. I just always assumed she'd die of old age. The alteration in my plan knocked me flat on my spiritual backside.

Footsteps on the stairs drew me away from my work.

Bryce padded towards me. "What's up?"

"Aren't you back from school early?"

"Skipped sports practice." He plopped into an unstable plastic chair across from me. "Welcome home to you too."

"You don't live here. Why would I say welcome home?" I knew what he meant, but sometimes sarcasm deserved a reply in kind. I went back to polishing the gear in my hand.

"Haven't you ever heard that home is where the heart is?" Teasing lightened his tone.

"Don't go getting all sentimental on me." If home was where the heart was, I had no idea where my home was. Not the house I grew up in. I missed it already, but without Mom or Dad there it didn't really matter. I loved Miss Lucy, but her apartment felt more like a home away from home. I loved Dad more than anyone else, but I doubted anyone could call wherever they were keeping him home.

"Earth to Heather." Bryce waved a hand in front of my face.

"Heaven," I said.

"Heaven?" He frowned. "You spaced out to heaven?"

"Home is where the heart is, right? Guess that means mine's in heaven."

"Oh." The confusion cleared off his face. "Yeah. Guess that's true." He nodded toward the disassembled press pieces scattered across the floor. "Can I help with something?"

"Can you do it without breaking anything?" I was only half joking. I didn't know where to find replacement parts if something broke.

He rolled his eyes and reached for the ancient tin oiling can. "I think I can handle it."

We sat in companionable silence, the ever-present dust motes swirling around us.

"Ready to pull an all-nighter?" I fitted two pieces back together. "Or do you need to get home?"

"I think I'm good for the all-night."

"Figured." I flashed him a smile. His parents considered his occasional spurts of going AWOL part of growing up. I wondered what they'd say if they knew their philosophy freed him for this type of work.

"So what's the goal?" Bryce asked.

"To get this thing printed." I pulled the crumpled draft out of my pocket and tossed it to him.

He smoothed it and scanned my cramped scribbles. Pressure and frustration had wreaked havoc on my normally neat handwriting.

"Too bad we can't include a picture."

"Hey!" I squeaked. "That's all you have to say about it?"

"It's good." He chuckled and tossed the paper back to me. "Even without a picture."

I stuffed the paper back into my pocket.

"So what comes next after we put this thing back together?" He used the oiling can to point at the frame of the press.

"We print the flyer."

"On what?"

"Paper." I resisted the urge to say "duh" and roll my eyes.

"Yeah. Obviously." He indulged in the dramatic eye-roll I had refrained from. "I mean, what paper. Where is it?"

"The boxes." I gestured toward the shelves. "Mom stockpiled it. People used to donate their paper ration to her."

Bryce rocked back on his heels and studied me.

"What?"

"Nothing." He looked away. "Which boxes?"

"No, I mean it. What was that look for?"

He shrugged. "You never talk about your mother."

"I don't usually use her press or hang out in her best friend's house either." I stood up to help him locate the right boxes. Talking about the paper hurt, but it didn't reach the aching pain buried deeper. I wasn't ready to go there. Not yet.

"Here it is." The cardboard box bore the word "PAPER" printed on the side of it. Mom's handwriting.

"How much is in it?" Bryce took the box off the shelf.

Water stains darkened the white cardboard. Not good. Not good at all. "I'm not sure. I don't think this box is any good."

"Why not?"

I tapped the brown blotch. "Water. Might still be useable, though. Let's find out."

Bryce plunked the box onto the work table and lifted the lid. "Um. Lots of paper but..."

I didn't want to look. "It's ruined?"

"Bluish-gray and kind of fuzzy."

"Definitely ruined." I pushed my hair back from my face. "What am I going to do? I should have checked on this before I started anything." This whole idea was stupid anyway. What made me think I could do it?

"Hey. Stop that." Bryce grabbed my shoulder and gave me a gentle shake. "You were focused on getting the press working. That's just as important."

"But useless without paper." I imagined Dad sitting alone in a jail cell, helpless. This was his chance. It was our chance.

"We'll get paper," Bryce said. "I'm pretty sure Miss Lucy knows how to recycle it."

"We need to get the posters out tomorrow, Bryce!" If government propagandists poisoned everyone with their lies before we published our side of the story, we wouldn't stand a chance.

"Okay. So we'll think of something and make it happen."

"Bryce, stop. This isn't even your thing. It's my idea and Miss Lucy already isn't sure about it."

"Miss Lucy wants you to be cautious," he said. "That's different from not being sure about it."

"Same difference to me."

"Stop interrupting." Bryce scowled. I almost told him I wasn't interrupting, but he kept going before I could get the words out. "You think I don't want to help your dad? You think you're the only one who cares what happens to him?"

"No. I never said that."

"Good. Because I do care what happens to him. And I think your idea is a good one." He waited for me to make eye contact. "I know it's risky, Heather. I'm not a dumb little kid. I can make choices for myself. And my choice is to help however I can."

"Bryce. No." I tried to force myself not to panic. Bryce wasn't Mom. This didn't have to end the same way.

"You know, you're kind of supposed to appreciate that." He smirked, teasing me, trying to coax a smile.

"Stop it."

"Come on." He grabbed my hand and pulled me off the floor.

"Where are we going?" I stumbled, trying not to step on the printing press parts.

"To get paper," he said.

I jerked my hand away. "I said no! You can't help me with this."

"But I'm going to." He turned to face me. "We're friends. You're basically my sister and your dad is more my dad than my real one is."

I shook my head. "You don't understand. It wouldn't make any difference if Dad was your real father. I still wouldn't want you to help me."

"Wait." His expression changed. He was fitting the pieces together. "This is about your mom, isn't it?"

"Don't. Just don't." I kept my volume steady even though I wanted to yell the words. Everything felt far too familiar. This little basement, the printing press, and my driving need to deliver something as dangerous as dynamite. My problem was I kept lighting the fuse and finding out someone I loved held the explosives.

"Heather," he stared at me, "things happen. We're Christians. Sometimes we die for that. Your Mom's death wasn't your fault."

"Yes, it was." If I hadn't pushed, we would have gone home instead of making the delivery. Mom would have spent that night safe in bed instead of bleeding her life out in a pitch-black alley.

Bryce shrugged. "Okay. Have it your way. But if anything happens to me, it definitely isn't your fault."

"If you get hurt helping me with my idea, it is definitely my fault."

"No." He shook his head. "Because now it's my idea too. And I'm going to keep working on it even if you quit. So it's not just yours. It's ours. We're partners."

"I don't want you to get hurt," I repeated. I loved Bryce. He was part of my family. One of the only people I had left. I couldn't stand the idea of anything happening to him.

"Me neither." He started up the stairs. "But God gets to make the call on that one. Not you. Not me."

That didn't leave me much room to argue. I jogged up the stairs to keep up. "Where are you going?"

"I already told you. I'm going to get paper."

Chapter Nine

"Where are you going to get paper? There's no paper just lying around waiting for us to grab it." We didn't have enough time to use Mom's method of collecting from Christians.

"Your confidence in me is touching. Really." Bryce smirked as he slid the hidden door shut and replaced the picture of the fawns.

"I don't have any problem with you. It's just..."

He cut me off. "Maybe you should stay here and finish putting the press back together. This doesn't really require two people."

"Forget it." I started shaking my head before he finished talking. Whatever he was planning, I wasn't going to stay behind. I couldn't let him go plowing into danger without backup.

"You don't even know what it is yet."

"Well then, start talking." I folded my arms. "Miss Lucy can finish cleaning the parts, and I can put the press together pretty fast."

He sighed. "It would be more efficient if you stayed here."

I glared at him until he broke eye contact. He ducked his head and left me scowling at a tangle of brown hair.

"What's going on?" Miss Lucy wheeled out of the kitchen and navigated towards us.

"The paper is ruined." I still felt like kicking myself. "I forgot to check on it."

"So now we're discussing where to get more." The couch sagged as Bryce sat down.

"I see." Miss Lucy raised her eyebrows at us. "And your plan is?"

Bryce jerked his thumb at me. "Keeping her out of trouble and making sure she doesn't quit." He turned to Miss Lucy. "Doing both at the same time might be a full time job."

Miss Lucy shook her head at him, eyes twinkling. "What's your plan, Heather?"

"I don't really know," I said. "I don't want anyone to get hurt helping me." Especially not Bryce. I didn't wish harm on anyone else either, but Bryce and Miss Lucy were the glue holding me together. If anything happened to them, I would crumble.

Miss Lucy gave me a smile that tilted the corners of her mouth down instead of up. She had loved Mom too. She understood.

"We need paper to make this work, and I know where to get some," Bryce said. "Heather's all worried about it though. She insists that if I go she's coming with me. It would be easier on my own."

"People went by twos a lot in the Bible," Miss Lucy said.

"But..."

Miss Lucy held up a hand to stop him. "I'm not saying it's always right. Just mentioning it."

"Okay." Bryce sat back, pacified.

"I've got to go with him," I said.

"I know." Miss Lucy shushed me with a wave of her hand. Her focus never left Bryce. "Where can you get paper?"

Bryce hesitated.

"You're going to have to tell me sooner or later." His reluctance made me more concerned about his plan.

"Fine." Bryce shrugged, but I could sense tension beneath his effort at nonchalance. "The government warehouse. I've got clearance."

"You can't be serious?" After venturing to the police station, I didn't want anything to do with another government building. We did need paper, though, and if Bryce went I was going too.

"How are you going to explain wanting a whole bunch of paper?" Miss Lucy asked.

"That's the easy part. I can say it's for my Dad. Or pull rank and tell the guards it's none of their business. Or say it's for a secret project." He ticked the options off on his fingers.

"Well, Heather," Miss Lucy turned to me. "What do you think?"

"I think it's crazy." I twisted my hair into a ponytail and tugged on it. "Do we have any other options?"

"Not that I can think of." She pursed her lips. "Not unless you want to abandon the idea."

I rubbed my temples. Mom would tell me to listen to God instead of fear. Dad ... I didn't know what Dad would tell me. I didn't even know what he thought about my choices the day Mom died. He said he didn't blame me, but I didn't think he approved of my decisions that day.

"C'mon, Heather." Bryce stood up. "You're not asking me. You're not making the call. It's my idea, and I want to do it."

"How much paper are you planning to get?" I stood too, a plan forming. As much as I wanted to go, Bryce was right. It was too dangerous for me to go just because I was worried about him. I needed a better reason.

"A box. Enough to get us started."

Miss Lucy nodded. "We can start collecting paper rations from the Christians if we need more later."

"How are you going to carry a whole box of paper on your bike by yourself?"

Bryce hesitated.

I could imagine him trying to balance the box on his handlebars and basket. It wouldn't work. Transporting something that heavy and awkward would be tricky even with two of us. But we could make it work.

"I can get someone else to help," he said.

I shook my head. "I don't want to pull anyone else into this. Especially not this early."

"Well I don't want you to get arrested before you even get started."

"I'll wear a disguise." Mom and I had sometimes done that to make deliveries where we might be recognized. "I saw my wig downstairs. I'm pretty sure it's still useable. And I can probably find Mom's dorky nerd glasses."

"Dorky nerd glasses?" Bryce raised his eyebrows.

I shrugged. "You'll see. The bottom line is, if anyone has seen pictures of me, I wasn't wearing them."

He still hesitated.

"You know you can't do it alone."

"Okay." He sighed. "Show me the disguise. If it's good enough, I think we can pull it off."

"I'll be praying the whole time you're gone," Miss Lucy said.

"Just act cool and confident." Bryce leaned his bike against the siding of a huge warehouse. "Whatever they say, we just brush them off. Like they're servants."

"I don't have any experience with servants, Bryce."

He shrugged. "You know from my stories. Play off that. You'll do fine."

I took a deep breath. If only I felt as confident as he sounded. If we botched this, it would be my fault. I swiped fake bangs away from my forehead

"You've got my back, right?" Bryce faced me and gave my shoulders a quick squeeze. I wondered if he could sense my apprehension.

"Always." If something did happen—something out of our control—I'd be glad I came. After all, the Bible did say two were better than one.

"Follow me." Bryce took off with a swaggering gate.

I hurried behind him, trying to decide how to match his confident appearance. I rarely saw this side of Bryce. This was his public persona, the cocky teenager who occasionally made screen appearances with his father.

As we made our way to the side door, the grass crackled under our feet. The stuff was either fake, dead, or some weird hybrid the government was testing. If it was the last option, I figured the experiment got an F.

Bryce swiped his card against a scanner embedded in the doorframe. The lock clicked open.

"Whoa. You can get in just like that? How much clearance do you have?"

"As much as I want." Bryce waved me inside and closed the door. We stood in a small, dark room. Clods of dirt covered the floor. Bryce turned the ID card towards me. His dad's picture stared unsmiling from beneath the shiny government seal. "I swiped his spare."

"But ... what if someone checks you?"

"Easy." He stuffed the card back into his pocket and pulled his own from the opposite side. "Left pocket Dad, right pocket me."

"Sneaky." I couldn't believe he walked around with the governor's spare ID card in his pocket.

"That's my middle name. Come on. I'd rather not bother with checking in, but the guard'll probably nab us anyway."

"Nab?" I grabbed his arm to keep him from walking away.

He rolled his eyes. "Make us sign in. Grouch at me for trying to break the rules. No big deal."

"Shouldn't we avoid bringing attention to ourselves that way?"

"Nah." Bryce smirked. "I've been trying to snitch stuff from this place since Dad took me for my first visit back when I was five. That's how the story goes anyway."

"You're insane."

"Part of the package when you're the governor's son." He rolled his eyes. "You're my girlfriend if they catch us. No one will question that. Now come with me." He leaned closer and whispered. "This is a game to me, remember. I have to act like it's hilarious."

"Okay. Got it." I willed my hands to stop trembling.

Bryce cracked the inside door open and light flooded the room. He peeked through before sticking his head out. I stood on my tiptoes to try to see past him. No luck.

"C'mon," Bryce hissed. He waved for me to follow without looking back. I jumped after him so fast I almost stepped on his heel.

We moved into a huge room. Steel shelves stretched to the ceiling like a city of sky scrapers.

Bryce tapped my shoulder and pointed up. Robotic arms hung from the support beams, scanning the room with security cameras. Bryce held a finger over his lips.

You couldn't have explained before? The cameras must be sound sensitive. At least, that was my first thought. I didn't dare whisper to Bryce to find out if I was right.

Bryce darted between two rows of shelving, crouched and scurrying on his tiptoes. I stood flatfooted a full two seconds after he took off.

He dropped down, rolled into a gap on the bottom shelf, and stuck his head out to grin at me.

I hurried after him. He grabbed my hand when I got close enough and pulled me onto the shelf with him. The bangs on my wig flopped into my eyes again.

"This is a game." His lips tickled my ear, his whisper almost too soft to make out the words. "No big deal if we get caught."

"I don't want to get caught," I whispered back.

He clapped a hand over my mouth. The gears of the closest robotic arm clicked above us.

"It can't see us." Bryce breathed into my ear.

I nodded to show I understood. His relaxed, playful attitude contrasted my pounding heart and desert-dry mouth. He rubbed my shoulder.

This was insane. We were going to end up in prison without doing Dad an ounce of good.

Bryce nudged me.

I glanced over my shoulder and gave him a "what?" look, afraid to say anything out loud. He made a shooing motion. He wanted me to get out.

I hesitated. I didn't like this place at all, but our shelf felt safer than the open aisle.

Bryce nudged harder.

Okay. Okay. I rolled off the shelf and crouched while Bryce unfolded himself.

He brushed sawdust off his shirt and winked.

"Bryce Williams." A voice boomed over the intercom system. "Stop right there."

I froze. They would recognize me for sure. They would arrest me. They might arrest Bryce just for being with me.

"Aw. C'mon." Bryce made an exaggerated shrug and glared at the camera that now pointed at us. "You could at least let me get a little farther before busting me."

"Sorry, kid. Come check in."

"Yeah, yeah. I'm coming." Bryce draped an arm around me and led me the opposite direction. He leaned close, a teasing smirk playing across his face. The teasing didn't quite reach his voice as he muttered. "You're my girlfriend. Right?"

I nodded and tried to smile back. "Is my hair on right?"

"Um," he glanced at me, "yeah. I can't get used to blond on you."

"Does it look fake?"

"Nah. You're fine." He tapped my nose teasingly, but his voice stayed serious. "You can be nervous, but at least try to look cool to impress your boyfriend, okay?"

"Okay." That part I thought I could handle. If no one recognized my face we might escape. I shot an arrow prayer to heaven, begging God not to let anyone realize my identity.

"This is so not fair." Bryce started complaining as we approached a huge wooden desk. I guessed it would take ten men to lift the thing. "So not fair." He continued. "You get all the gadgets to catch me and what do I get? Nothing. It's not right."

"Sign in, kid." The guard seemed annoyed. Or was he amused? I couldn't tell.

"I know. I know." Bryce reached into his right pocket and flipped his dad's ID onto the counter.

"And the girl's."

"Aw, man, gimme a break." Bryce whined. "We've only been going for a few weeks. I promised this gig wouldn't get her in any trouble. Nothing on the record, you know?"

"Protocol—"

Bryce interrupted. "Protocol nothing. When a work crew comes in you don't make every single guy sign in. Just the boss. I'm the boss, okay."

Agree, I begged silently, *let us get away with this.*

The guard cursed under his breath. "You are a pain in the..."

"I know. I know." Bryce chuckled and scribbled his name onto the sign-in screen.

I stared at the sloppy letters, now saved where any government worker with clearance could see. Bryce's name was now connected to this place at this time. How long would it take for someone to put the pieces together?

"What did you come for?" The guard asked.

"Paper." Bryce grabbed my hand. "For a competition. We're going to make everyone jealous."

The guard looked skeptical.

"You wouldn't understand. But no one else will be able to get as much as us, so we'll make the biggest splash for sure."

"I don't know..."

Bryce rolled his eyes and towed me away from the desk. "We'll be out of your hair in a couple minutes. We only need one box."

One box. Five thousand sheets of paper. More than enough to keep us busy for a week. We could spread our posters around most of the neighborhoods. If we stretched them thin, we might even penetrate the main city.

"One box?!" The guard's eyes widened.

Bryce didn't stop to explain. He didn't even bother to look back. He just laughed and started jogging down the first aisle.

Chapter Ten

The next morning I jolted into a sitting position before I even registered the buzzing alarm. I swung my legs over the side of the bed and slapped it off.

In the silence after the sound died away, I could hear Bryce moving around in the living room. Today we entered phase two. Distribution. It made the risk of yesterday's escapade to the warehouse seem small.

I fumbled in the dark for my bag, biting back a yelp as my head collided with the bed post.

For once I was glad most of my clothing was black. I identified a pair of pants and a shirt by feel, no worries about making them match.

I slipped out of my pajamas and wiggled into the clean outfit. My leather jacket hung on the other bed post. I grabbed it, located my boots, and headed down the hall.

"That you?" Bryce whispered as I felt my way into the living room.

"It's me. Is it okay to turn on the lights or will it drain the battery too much?

"The battery would work fine, but it's not public knowledge that Miss Lucy has one."

"Never mind then. Do you have the flyers?"

He didn't respond, so I figured he must have nodded. "Bryce, I can't see you."

"Sorry." I could hear rueful amusement in his voice. "Yes, I have the flyers. You ready?"

"Whenever you are."

"Let's go then."

I followed the sound of his footsteps across the room and down the entrance hall. When we slipped out the door, I walked to the middle of the road and tipped my head back, picking out constellations in the strip of sky between the tenement buildings. The Milky Way mirrored our tiny alley. I smiled as I turned my attention back to the task at hand.

Pin-pricks of light from the stars and the soft glow of the moon lessened the intensity of the darkness, but I still struggled to make out shadowy shapes of objects and buildings.

"Dark, isn't it?" Bryce said.

"You can say that again."

"Dark, isn't it?" he repeated.

I smacked him and bit back a giggle when he jumped.

"Hey!" he protested. "You invited me to say it again."

"It was rhetorical, and you know it."

He led the way over to his bike and tucked the stack of papers into a pouch strapped to the handle bars.

"Can you see well enough to ride?" I asked.

"I do it every morning." He flipped the kickstand up. "Hop on."

I obeyed, and Bryce shoved off. He coasted out of the alley and turned left.

The first glow of light began to show as we entered an area I recognized. Bryce followed the main street for a ways, then started weaving through a series of back roads.

My sense of direction disappeared somewhere along the maze of streets. By the time he braked, I had no idea where we were.

We jumped off the bike, and Bryce took the papers out of the pouch.

"Here." He reached into his jacket pocket and handed me a tiny box of tacks and a bottle of glue.

"You think people will see them here?" We had stayed up almost the entire night before crashing, but set up had delayed us a long time. We only had three hundred flyers to distribute today. I wanted every single one of them to count. We needed people to start talking. We needed them to doubt the government and care what happened to Dad.

"I'm sure of it." He pointed down the road. "There's one main road down there and another one at the other end. People cut across here all the time."

We moved to an old telephone pole, gray, splintered with age and riddled with staples left from the days paper notices were still common.

I opened the box of tacks, handed one to Bryce and watched while he fastened two flyers to the pole.

We moved down the street quickly, placing flyers in obvious places but making sure they were well spaced. When we finished the street, we returned to Bryce's bicycle.

An hour later, about thirty flyers remained. Enough to do one more street. The two hundred and seventy already posted felt like a great victory, but a nagging voice of doubt warned me that it would never be enough. Two hundred and seventy pieces of paper could never create a big enough splash to even garner government attention. The idea that we might create enough stir to influence what happened to Dad was ludicrous.

Bryce straddled his bike. "Should we risk another street or head home?"

I hesitated. The sun was creeping higher in the sky. People moved about in some of the houses.

"What do you think?" I asked.

"It's up to you."

Fine lot of help that was. I sighed. I wanted to keep going, but my cautious side won out. "Let's head back."

Bryce nodded. "I think that's a good idea."

We didn't venture onto the main streets as we started home. Both of us were all too aware of the remaining flyers in the bike pouch. As we passed one of the streets we'd stopped on earlier, a flyer blew across the street in front of us.

"Bryce! Stop."

He slammed the brakes on and put his foot down fast to keep from tipping over. "What's wrong?"

I jogged to the flyer and picked it up, then raised it for Bryce to see. "It must have fallen off."

His shoulders sagged. "Heather, you scared me."

"Sorry."

"It wouldn't hurt to just leave it, you know," he said. "Someone's just as likely to pick it off the ground as notice it on a telephone pole."

True enough. Old newspaper scraps that occasionally found their way onto the streets drew lots of attention.

"Should I just leave it?"

Bryce stiffened a moment before the sound reached me. A motor. I darted a glace towards the sun. It was still pretty low in the sky. Maybe high enough for a small car to operate off of, but I doubted it. That meant it had to be a government car.

"Heather, come on!" Bryce hissed.

I registered his words, but didn't move, unable to decide if I should stuff the paper in my pocket or drop it.

"C'mon." He begged. The rumble of the motor came closer. I saw the car round the corner, government insignia emblazoned across the hood.

I dropped the paper and darted to the bike, almost tipping it over as I leapt onto the passenger pegs.

Bryce steadied it, then stood up on the pedals, throwing his entire body into forcing the bike into motion. A gust of wind caught the poster and pinned it against the curb.

A honk from the car made me jump, upsetting the balance of the bike again.

"Stay still, would you?" Bryce grunted as he fought to keep the bike upright and moving. The honk was probably a signal for us to stop, but Bryce didn't even hesitate.

I tightened my death grip on his shoulders and twisted to look behind me. Bryce could bike like I could run, but I didn't see how we could beat a car.

"Stay still!" Bryce shouted.

The car gained ground on us. I wondered how long it would take for them to realize I was Rayford Stone's daughter. By now they must know I was the one who took the Bible from the sorting center.

The car began to slow. The passenger door opened, and a uniformed man stooped to pick up the flyer. A second man stepped from the driver's door and lifted a dark box to his eye.

"Turn around," Bryce growled, huffing the words as he panted for breath.

I obeyed, but I still saw the flash of light. A moment later, I realized what the box was. A camera. The driver had taken a picture of us.

Bryce leaned into a turn, and this time I leaned with him.

He sped to the next side road. "What happened?"

"They stopped to pick up the flyer," I said. "Bryce, they took a picture of us."

"Hang on." The back tire skidded as he raced into another turn. After straightening the bike, he glanced over his shoulder at me. "Nothing we can do about it."

Bryce reached the edge of the slums before he slowed. He coasted into a tiny alley behind a cluster of shanties. We got off. He leaned the bike against a rusted sheet of metal before collapsing next to it.

I sat down next to him. "I'm sorry, Bryce. I'm really sorry." Sorry didn't change anything, but I didn't know what else to say.

He shook his head, pulling his knees to his chest and gasping for breath.

"Don't tell me it's not my fault," I said. "We're both old enough to know it is."

He shook his head again and held his hand up, signaling for me to wait until he caught his breath.

I wrapped my arms around my middle and leaned forward a little, trembling as my adrenaline level sank. After a lifetime of avoiding government officials, I'd been chased by police twice in one week.

"It's not your fault," Bryce said after he caught his breath enough to talk.

"Yes, it is. You know it is."

"You froze. You couldn't help it."

"I couldn't decide what to do with the paper. I ... I don't know..."

He nodded. "Crazy thing to have happen our very first time out."

"They got a picture."

"Like I said. We can't do anything about it." He sighed. "I wonder if Dad pays enough attention to know what kind of bike I have."

"Plenty of boys have brown hair and ride that kind of bike. And my body probably blocked you pretty well." My stomach twisted. If Bryce's dad suspected anything, if he made the connection, the record from the warehouse would confirm everything. "Would your Dad suspect you?"

"He prides himself on being impartial."

"Won't he assign investigation to people under him? Maybe he won't even see the picture."

"He'll see it." Bryce sighed again and stretched. I looked at him, searching for a glimpse of emotion. His nonchalance didn't fool me, and his eyes couldn't hide his pain.

"Bryce..." I touched his arm, not sure what to say. What words of comfort could you give to someone whose own father might kill him if the truth ever surfaced?

"Knowing Dad, he's going to make our flyers his personal project as soon as he finds out about them." A hint of bitterness spiced the words. "He'll see the picture."

"You shouldn't go home." If Governor Williams put the pieces together while Bryce was home. I didn't want to think about it.

"Don't you ever read those old books you sort?"

I frowned. How did that question relate to the topic at hand? Once in a while, I read a book for fun. Mostly I smuggled Christian books out and read them at home.

"I like old mysteries," Bryce said. "Mom gets them for me sometimes. The legal ones. In a mystery, everyone suspects the person who runs away from the scene of a crime. If I don't go home, it'll lead Dad right to me."

I nodded, but in my heart, I still didn't want him to go.

Chapter Eleven

As we resumed our ride back to Miss Lucy's, I couldn't move my thoughts away from the threat of Bryce's father seeing that picture.

Reed Williams, governor of the North-Eastern Region, carried a long-standing grudge against Christians. Like Saul in the Bible, he seemed driven and adept at finding and punishing us. I could only imagine how furious he would be to discover his own son had converted several years ago.

Bryce had lived with that concern for years, afraid of his father learning the truth, but also harboring a deep shame for not sharing the Good News with his own parents. He and Dad had talked about his concern for his parents many times. Bryce vacillated between thinking he was a coward and feeling convinced he shouldn't risk bringing his father's wrath down on the Christian underground with renewed force.

"Ssst! Hey! Hey you." A boy stepped out from a narrow gap between two houses. "Wait up."

Bryce hesitated, glancing behind us, before braking. "What do you want?"

As he got closer, I recognized him as the boy we'd gone past on our way into the slums. Alden. Up close he looked even more like a waif. Dirt streaked his face, and his blond hair looked like it hadn't been washed in a week.

"Seen you coming and going an awful lot. Ain't never stopped to say hi to me."

"Sorry." Bryce smiled. "I've had a lot on my mind."

"You fretting on that dude what's got arrested?"

"Pardon?" A note of caution entered Bryce's voice. "I'm not sure what you mean."

"The screen man. Rayford Stone. Y'know. The one they say goes with that rebel group. The ones that call themselves Christians." Alden's slang and mannerisms made him seem older than he looked. I wondered how much of the street talk was natural and how much was an attempt to seem tough and grown-up.

Bryce shrugged. "I'm not sure he did anything wrong, but I haven't been crying over it."

I'd done enough crying for both of us.

"Where'd you get the girl?" Alden pointed at me.

Bryce backpedaled to get better leverage on the bike. "She's my girlfriend."

I resisted the urge to touch my wig. It was still in place, right? And the glasses perched on my nose.

"I don't like her," Alden said. "You should dump her."

Bryce rolled his eyes. "I'm seventeen. You're what, eight? No offense, but I'm not dumping my favorite girlfriend on your say-so."

"You got more than one?" Alden's eyes gleamed. I could imagine him impressing his friends with a story about this big kid with multiple girlfriends.

I tapped Bryce on the shoulder. "I really need to get home."

"Yeah." Bryce slid back onto the seat of his bike. "I'm sorry, Alden, but we really do have to..."

Alden reached into the giant cargo pocket on his oversized cargo shorts and pulled out a pocket screen. "Wait."

"If you're going to show me a picture of..." Bryce trailed off as Alden shoved the screen at him.

Where did a kid like Alden get a school screen? I wondered if the screen was stolen. Or maybe Alden went to school for a few days just to get one.

I peered over his shoulder and caught my breath. A capture of one of our posters filled the screen.

"One of my friends sent me that," he said.

"So?" Bryce shrugged. I hoped the boy didn't notice the tremor in his voice.

"So, you keep going in and out at all the right times."

Bryce flicked Alden's screen off. "It's really none of your business."

"Who says?"

Bryce tousled his hair and earned a glare.

"Look kid," he said, "I know the police don't come here much, but they wouldn't like that picture. You should delete it. School screens get monitored."

"Police won't bother me none," Alden scoffed. "I ain't no Christian man."

"You ain't no government man either." Bryce leaned down to Alden's level. He waited for Alden to look at him. "Living here doesn't make you invincible. You know that, right?"

"I can take care of myself."

"Bryce." I put a foot on one of the passenger pegs. "We really need to go."

"Yeah," Bryce looked at Alden, "we do. You be careful, okay?"

"Sure." Alden stepped out of our way. "I still wanna know 'bout you and those posters though."

"Nothing to know." Bryce pushed off. "We're being careful just like you should."

I could feel Alden watching us as Bryce peddled away.

"I don't like that," I said after we left him behind. "He asked too many questions."

"He's eight. And he lives here." Bryce shrugged. "The second the kids think they know you, they look for every potential tidbit of gossip. I just hope he doesn't get in trouble for flashing that photo around."

"I hope he doesn't get us in trouble flashing it around."

"Doesn't matter so much for us, does it? I mean, spreading the news is kind of the point, right?"

"I guess." Something seemed wrong, though. Alden was making connections we didn't want made. "I don't trust him."

"Neither do I," Bryce didn't sound as worried as I felt. "But as long as we keep not trusting him, I think we'll be fine."

The door to Miss Lucy's apartment swung open before Bryce could set the kickstand. Miss Lucy waited in the doorway, silent until we reached her. "Are you two all right?"

We exchanged a glance.

"Yeah," I said. "We're fine."

Bryce scanned the street. "Let us in, huh? Is something wrong?"

She wheeled her chair back. "Three messengers have come in the past half hour to tell me that ten blocks in the city have been closed off with a warning about terrorist activity."

"It wasn't terrorists." I closed the door behind us.

"We had some trouble," Bryce said. "We got caught. Sort of. Government people saw us, but they stopped to pick up a flyer we dropped, and we got away."

"But they got a picture of us." I sagged against the wall. My heart went back to racing as I thought through the events of the morning.

"These close calls can't become a habit." Miss Lucy waggled a finger at us.

"I'm not too fond of them myself," I said. *Understatement of the year.* Running away from the cops transporting Dad had been more than enough danger to fill my quota for a good long time. "Does this mean no one got our flyers?"

"First things first," Miss Lucy rolled into the living room. "Right now you should just be thanking God you made it back here in one piece."

"No kidding." Bryce sank onto the floor, sitting cross-legged. "I thought we were goners on our first mission."

I tossed the extra flyers onto the coffee table and dropped next to Bryce.

"Heather's right though," Bryce continued. "I doubt anyone outside of the government got those flyers."

Miss Lucy handed us glasses of ice water. "In that case, the government workers must be the people who needed to see the flyers."

I sighed. Looking on the bright side of everything twenty-four-seven could get annoying.

"What do you plan to do next?" she asked.

I tilted my cup to make the water swish. The ice cubes clinked against the glass. I didn't know what to tell her.

"I think right now the plan is to regroup and make a plan," Bryce said.

I shot him a grateful smile.

"Ain't easy to stick to a plan when everything is so uncertain." Miss Lucy patted my arm. "No shame in admitting that."

Someone pounded on the door in the rhythmic knock of a messenger.

Bryce stood. "We know about the flyers already. And the road blocks too," he grumbled.

He returned a few moments later with Ansley trailing behind him. She waved at me and smiled a little, gasping for breath. I felt a twinge of guilt for never getting a replacement Bible to her. Thank God we never had a chance to pass the little red one along to her, though. It would have led the Agency right to her.

"Is this about the road blocks?" Miss Lucy asked.

Ansley shook her head.

Miss Lucy and Bryce exchange a glance. I couldn't tell if they looked concerned or puzzled.

"Here, Ansley, sit down." I stood up and gestured at the couch.

"Thanks." She sagged into the seat.

"So what happened?" Bryce's words came out fast and forceful.

"They got a picture of Heather."

"A good one? I mean, we know they took one but we weren't sure how well it would come out." We needed people to link me to the posters. They needed to know Dad's death affected more than one person. But...

"That's not what I mean." Ansley pressed a hand against her chest and took a few deep breaths. "They matched the picture they took this morning with a portrait of you from your house."

"What about Bryce?" Everyone seemed concerned about the picture of me, but I didn't understand what difference that made. They already knew my name and what I looked like. If that wasn't enough, my name and age were plastered on the posters we had distributed. My role in the underground was unquestionable at this point.

"Nothing in the main database," Ansley said. "Yet."

Bryce frowned. "I'm sure Dad would recognize me from the picture."

"Just count your blessings," I said.

"I'd be happy to if I didn't think it was a trick." His forehead wrinkled. "If I didn't know better, I'd say Dad was trying to protect his reputation."

Ansley spoke before I could ask Bryce what he meant.

"Do you plan to make more flyers?" She held up a stack of blank paper. "Carmen gave me this. And if you make more, I can recruit some other messengers to help distribute them."

I hesitated. I didn't want to pull more people into this. But having the option to spread out more would increase the chance of success. If one neighborhood kept quiet, maybe a different one would start talking.

I rubbed the back of my neck. Talking wasn't going to save Dad. I wasn't even sure outrage could save him, and I couldn't remember the last time injustice had evoked outrage from anyone except the people directly affected.

"Do you really think this is worth it?" I asked. I looked around the room.

Ansley nodded. "Laying low isn't getting us anywhere."

"And this is?" I tried to sound pragmatic. The last thing I wanted was all of them trying to comfort me and convince me there was still hope. I knew all the verses and sayings already. "The flyers probably won't make anything happen. And they'll put everyone involved in the project in danger."

"We're all in danger anyway." Bryce spoke quietly. "Ansley's right. Right now my dad is in charge mostly because he's good at keeping people happy and making sure the people over him don't have to bother with this region."

"Exactly." That supported my fears. "He's good at maintaining status quo and keeping revolutionaries quiet."

"And normal people don't challenge that because they don't know there's anything to rebel about."

Ansley nodded. "I'm in danger anyway. I take risks every time I run messages. But everything I'm doing right now just maintains status quo."

"Point being?" I was losing this conversation. They weren't going to let themselves off the hook.

"Point being, I want to be part of making things change."

"And you think this is going to make something change?"

Ansley shrugged. "Maybe. Our neighbors are self-centered, but they're not cruel."

Ansley lived closer to the main city, in a ritzier area than I did.

"She's right." Bryce nodded. He lived right on the border of the main city. The richest place you could get. "You should hear how distraught my mom's friends get over kicked puppies."

"Kicked puppies?" I frowned.

"Figure of speech." He shrugged. "Stray animals. Cute kids. They're still self-centered about it, but they can't resist a good sob story."

Great. Dad was getting reduced to a good sob story.

Ansley gave me an encouraging smile. "What we're trying to say is that we think people will listen if we can just get the story to them. We can't know for sure how they'll react. But it's worth a try."

"Do you think it matters? Will the government react to the people if the people care what happens to Dad?"

"Maybe." Bryce started pacing. "We've got the advantage that your dad is already a public figure. People like him from the live cast. They already care what happens to him. They're looking for answers."

"If they think the government is lying to them..." Ansley said.

Miss Lucy continued the thought. "Or if they think the government is trying to steal someone they enjoy..."

"They might just get mad," Ansley finished.

"And if they get mad," Bryce paused, frowning thoughtfully, "Dad might do what it takes to keep them quiet. He might preserve the status quo to keep word from getting to his superiors and having his position questioned."

"We might actually cause the first big concern the government offices have felt in a long time." Miss Lucy's eyes sparkled.

I looked around the room and found her excitement mirrored on Bryce and Ansley's faces. Bryce was right. This wasn't just my thing anymore. I didn't like it. I didn't like feeling so scared and responsible. I couldn't argue with their logic, though. Their reasoning gave me hope that we had a chance.

"Onward then." I stood up and offered my hand to Bryce.

"Onward Christian soldiers." He hoisted himself off the floor.

The next morning Ansley showed up with two other messengers. We divided eight-hundred flyers between the five of us.

"Heather?" Ansley waited until the other three messengers turned and began disappearing into the darkness. "Are you sure you should help with the distribution?"

"Why wouldn't I?"

"You're kind of our leader now. What if something happened to you?"

I froze. I didn't want that title. I didn't want any more responsibility. "I'm not your leader. I'm just trying to get Dad out of prison."

"Which makes you our leader."

I opened my mouth, another protest ready on my lips, but I bit it back. "Good leaders don't ask people to take risks they aren't willing to take themselves."

"We all know you're willing."

I shook my head and gave her a quick hug. "I need something to do, Ansley. I can't stay cooped up inside all day every day. I'll go insane."

"Insane leaders tend to be counterproductive." Even with the darkness hiding his face, Bryce's tone made his teasing obvious. He was good at lightening the mood when I started stressing. I doubted he felt very cheerful himself, so I appreciated the effort.

Ansley squeezed my arm. "Be careful."

"We will."

"And even if she won't, I will," Bryce added.

Ansley backed away, her hand silhouetted in a wave.

Chapter Twelve

We handed out all three hundred of our flyers without incident. The build-up of sleepless nights, pressure, and the tension of sneaking around with the flyers left me feeling drained. I tried to focus on the sense of accomplishment instead.

In a world that rarely saw paper, three hundred flyers was a major accomplishment. If people wanted answers about Dad, they would flock to our unique way of broadcasting the story. It could work. I kept trying to convince myself it could.

Bryce's posture began to relax as we reached the edge of the slums. He slowed the even but hurried pace he'd been maintaining for the past twenty minutes.

"I hope the others didn't run into trouble," I said.

"Me too." He sounded distant.

"What are you thinking about?"

"Dad." He shrugged. "And Mom."

Miss Lucy had taken my side the previous night. Bryce hadn't returned home. We had worked the press in silence through the midnight hours. His misery made my heart ache.

I knew what it was like to lose a parent. The pain from losing Mom still felt suffocating at times. I couldn't imagine how horrible Bryce must feel to live in fear of his own father.

He was so lost in thought, he didn't slow when Alden walked out of Miss Lucy's alley.

"Bryce." I tapped his shoulder and smiled at Alden.

Alden didn't return the gesture. His eyes widened when he saw us. I let my hand drop as he scooted around the corner and ran away.

"Weird." Bryce watched him as he disappeared into another alley. "If I know anything about the kids here, he's up to no good."

"Why would he even be here?" I hopped off the passenger pegs as Bryce stopped the bike. He pushed it to the side of the road and set the kickstand.

"Let's walk. Just in case," he said.

"Yeah." I hugged myself. *I will trust, and not be afraid.*

"Stay behind me." Bryce put out his arm to hold me back.

I smiled in spite of myself. Sometimes I thought Bryce mistook himself for my father instead of my friend. My father or ... something else. Heat rose to my face, and I darted a glance at Bryce. He wasn't looking at me. Thank goodness he couldn't hear my thoughts.

We peered around the corner together. I felt like a spy from the exaggerated propaganda clips the government produced.

Bryce cursed under his breath, a rare occurrence.

"What?" I tried to see around him, but he pushed me back.

"Stop it." I ducked under his arm to get a better look. Miss Lucy's door hung crooked on its hinges. A cop pushed it aside and ducked through the gap.

Bryce backed into me, and I stumbled.

"Where's Miss Lucy?" I steadied myself on the wall.

He turned his palms up and shrugged

Several more police came out of the house. They headed in our direction.

"Heather!" Bryce dragged me away. We ran to the next alley and slipped down it just as the police emerged onto the main street.

"What if they have Miss Lucy?" I watched them file down the street. None of them seemed to be carrying anything or anyone. "They must have her."

"Maybe someone sent her a message." He kept a restraining hand on my shoulder. It wasn't necessary. I knew better than to single-handedly attack a bunch of cops. My failure to rescue Dad was still far too fresh to allow for any heroics.

When the last of the police disappeared around a corner, I stepped forward.

"Wait!" Bryce grabbed me back again.

"Stop doing that."

"There might be more of them."

I shrugged. "Maybe. Maybe not."

"Better safe than sorry," he shot back.

I gritted my teeth. "We need to find out what happened to Miss Lucy."

"Shh." He held a finger to his lips.

"Don't shush..."

He put his hand over my mouth. I considered licking him until I heard the rhythmic thump of running feet. A moment later, Ansley ran by our hiding place.

"Hey!" Bryce jumped out, his voice a whispered yell.

Ansley spun around.

I joined Bryce. "Something's happened. The police broke into Miss Lucy's place."

"I'm too late." She grimaced and braced her hands on her knees.

"What this time?" We pulled her back into the alley, away from prying eyes. I hoped. I glanced over my shoulder, checking for children sticking their noses where they didn't belong.

"I don't really know." Ansley leaned against the brick wall, chest still heaving. "I stopped at Carmen's when I finished my flyers and she was in a panic. She sent me to tell you the police were on the way and you had to leave quick. Something about a spy and the government warehouse."

"You signed your name." I turned to Bryce. "Your dad must know."

Bryce nodded, his shoulders slumping. "I guess so. What about the spy?"

"I bet it was Alden," I said.

Bryce shook his head. "No way, he's only..."

"Stop." I cut him off. "You just don't want it to be true."

"Who's Alden?" Ansley cocked an eyebrow at us.

"A kid from around here. Not even ten," Bryce said. "There's no way he could be the spy."

"Why not?" Ansley glanced at me. "What makes you think it's him?"

"He was here," I said. "He left right before the police came out of the house."

"Does he normally hang around here?"

Bryce shook his head slowly. "No. Not really. But he probably just followed the police to get a good story for his friends."

He was grasping at thin air and coming up empty. We all knew slum kids gave the police a wide berth whenever possible.

"I'll tell Carmen that Alden's our prime suspect for the spy," Ansley said. "You'll have to ask her about the warehouse. She said something about a recording from there. Maybe the security camera record or something."

I stepped out of the alley and peered around the corner. The street was still clear. No sign of more police. "We need to check on Miss Lucy."

"Heather," Bryce put a hand on my shoulder, "she didn't get any warning."

"I know." I swallowed past a lump in my throat. "I just have to see."

Miss Lucy had warned me to be careful. She told me to let the paint dry on my half-baked idea before taking action. Maybe if I had listened better, she would still be okay. Just like Mom would still be okay if I had thought for more than thirty seconds before insisting on a dangerous idea.

"Let me go first." Bryce pushed by me and stepped out of the alley.

Ansley and I followed him.

I will trust, and not be afraid: for the Lord Jehovah is my strength and my song.

We crept toward the house, listening for any sounds that might indicate lingering intruders. We heard nothing. The silence gave the street an eerie feel.

Bryce gestured for us to stay back as he approached the door. He pried it open just enough to slip inside. The bent hinges grated together.

"Miss Lucy?" Bryce called.

I followed him, heart in my throat. I didn't want to find Miss Lucy's body. The very thought made my stomach revolt. But I had to know.

I shuddered as we stepped into the living room. It looked like our house after the agency police arrested Dad. The coffee table lay on its side, one leg shattered. Stuffing bubbled out of a slash in the couch.

Bryce glanced around the room. "Miss Lucy?"

Ansley headed down the hallway. I heard her checking the bedrooms. She stepped into the kitchen on her way back.

"No sign of her." She announced. "No wheelchair either."

"Would they have taken the wheelchair when they arrested her?" Bryce scanned the debris as if searching for an answer.

I shook my head. How should I know? The paralyzed sensation gripped me again. My thoughts refused to focus. My fault. All of this was my fault.

Bryce sank to his knees. He lifted a cross stitch off the floor and brushed debris off it. The footprint of a boot refused to be brushed off the delicate stitching portraying a pair of shy fawns.

"I wonder what they'll do with her." Ansley righted the coffee table. A futile gesture. After we left, I doubted any of us would ever return. The furniture would either remain to collect dust and cobwebs or be cleared out by squatters.

"She's too old to be arrested again." Last time they arrested her, when she was young, she escaped with her life but without the use of her legs. This time...

My throat constricted.

"She's stronger than you think." Bryce stood up, cradling the cross-stitch. "We'll have to add her story to the posters."

I shook my head. "I'm done with that."

They both stared at me.

"This is..." I trailed off, staring at the frame in Bryce's hands. Those fawns. They used to hang over the latch to the hidden door.

My heart sped. I glanced towards the door. Still closed. Would police bother to close it behind them if they had discovered it? I glanced around the trashed room and came to the obvious conclusion. The door would be open if they had found it. Was it possible?

"What is it?" Bryce waved a hand in front of my face.

I scrambled across the room, hopping around toppled furniture. "The basement!"

Bryce beat me to the secret door. He dragged it open and peered into the darkness.

"It's about time." Miss Lucy's voice echoed up the stairs.

My legs almost buckled.

Bryce raced down the stairs. "What happened? Miss Lucy, where...?"

135

I heard a loud crash, and Miss Lucy gave a little shriek. A moment later Bryce groaned. I peered into the darkness but couldn't see either one of them.

"Mind your feet, boy," Miss Lucy scolded.

"Are you okay?" I called.

I heard Bryce moving around again. "I'm so sorry," he said. "What happened?"

The light flicked on.

Miss Lucy sat at the bottom of the stairs, propped against her tipped wheelchair. Bryce must have tripped over her.

I jogged down, relieved to be making the journey with light. As I got closer, I could see bruises on her face and arms.

"What happened, Miss Lucy? Are you okay?" I knelt next to her.

"I'm fine, child. Just fine. A bit banged up, but nothing time won't heal."

Bryce squatted next to me. "What happened?"

"One of the neighbors came by to tell me police were heading my way. I knew I couldn't get out, so I folded up my wheelchair, pushed it down here, and did my best to follow it."

Bryce and I stared at her, not sure what to say.

"Got these bruises because I couldn't quite figure out how to maneuver the stairs." She gave a rueful smile. "I ended up tumbling down most of them."

"But you're okay?" Bryce asked.

"Just fine."

"What should we do?" He picked her up with a grunt and started up the stairs.

"We need to get ourselves out of here and bring as many supplies as possible with us."

I trailed them up the stairs, relieved but still sick to my stomach over the tragedy I'd almost caused. What now? How could we continue?

Bryce set Miss Lucy down on the damaged couch. "I'll go back and see if your wheelchair is still useable."

"Thank you."

She smiled at me and patted the couch beside her. "Sit down, child. You look like you've seen a ghost."

"I kind of feel like I'm seeing one." I sat down next to her. "We thought we'd lost you for sure."

"I'm still here and still kicking." She chuckled. "I wonder if they've realized who this apartment belongs to yet."

I gave her a quizzical look.

"They've pretty much ignored me since they let me out of prison." She picked at the yellow foam coming out of the armrest. "Carmen says they don't keep good records on people in the slums. I wonder if they'll make the connection between me and the girl they arrested all those years ago."

"I hope they don't," I said. Miss Lucy was the person everyone had expected me to follow after. Years ago, in her early twenties, she had tried to bring about change. Her efforts hadn't gone far. A handful of people got saved, but the Agency had arrested her quickly and assured everyone that she was rogue revolutionary.

I realized that Dad's arrest had pushed me into fulfilling those expectations. I was walking in her footsteps more closely than I ever expected.

Miss Lucy smiled and patted the cushion she sat on. "I think this old thing has earned retirement, don't you?"

"Maybe."

"Heather." Miss Lucy scooted closer and put her arm around me. "No one got arrested or hurt. God protected all of us."

"I know."

"What's wrong then, honey?" She gave my shoulders a little squeeze.

I shrugged. "I don't think this is going to be enough for Dad. And now with this happening to you. It's only a matter of time before they start catching us."

"Leading something like this is a lot of responsibility."

I sighed and nodded. "Sometimes it feels like too much responsibility."

Bryce clomped up the stairs, carrying the wheelchair with him. "One of the handles is bent and the frame is dinged up, but I think it'll work."

"Wonderful." Miss Lucy gave me another hug before turning to look at her chair.

"What now?" Bryce asked.

"You two go disassemble the printing press and get any flyers that haven't been distributed. If you can get me into my chair, I'll go gather some little things I don't want the police getting their hands on."

I gasped and scrambled to my feet. "The police! Dad's Bible."

"I thought of that already," Miss Lucy said. "It's hidden in my room. I was afraid I'd ruin it if I tried to get it downstairs. I doubt they found it."

"I'll meet you downstairs." Bryce picked his way through the littered room. "We should hurry. Don't want to be here if they come back."

Ansley helped us pack the press and a few other things onto the wheelchair. Bryce would carry Miss Lucy.

"Carmen said she'd meet us at my house," Ansley said. "My parents know about everything, and they want to put you up temporarily."

I hated the idea of dragging more people into this. But we couldn't stay here.

"Maybe it's time for me to take to the streets," I said.

"Nonsense." Ansley waved her hand as if batting my words away. "You're coming home with me. If you feel the need, you're welcome to fight it out with my parents. But you'll lose."

Doubtless true. Winning arguments with her lawyer father was harder than locating and smuggling Bibles.

"We'll come. We need a place to unload my chair if nothing else," Miss Lucy said.

Bryce nodded and picked her up. "We'll stick to back roads as much as possible."

I hesitated as they stepped outside.

Ansley stopped beside me and patted my arm. "No use crying over spilt milk."

"This isn't spilt milk." I scanned the room. "I'm putting people's lives in danger."

She shrugged and started maneuvering the wheelchair towards the door. "I think this is a lot bigger than you."

"It's still my fault."

Ansley ignored me. She lifted the wheelchair over the threshold and joined Bryce on the street.

I lingered a moment longer. Coming here had felt like coming home. Now I was losing this place, too. From now on, there would be no home to retreat to.

My skin prickled as I stepped outside. I glanced at the windows facing the street like dozens of spying eyes. "Maybe we should break up."

Ansley glanced over her shoulder. "What do you mean?"

"I mean we're about as conspicuous as an elephant."

Bryce nodded. "Heather and I both know the way to your place. You two can take the wheelchair. Me and Miss Lucy'll meet you over there."

Ansley nodded. "Okay. Works for me."

I nodded my agreement.

"Sounds good." He turned left and started down an even smaller alley between two of the tenements. "See you there."

"Do the others know what's going on?" I asked as we started in the opposite direction.

"Most of the messengers know by now that Miss Lucy is okay, and that we're moving you guys to my house. They're spreading the word through the network right now."

"That's good," I said, but I couldn't help thinking how much time it took away from printing and distributing flyers. "It's not going to work, is it?"

"Depends on what you're talking about." Ansley glanced at me.

"Getting Dad out."

She shrugged. "I don't think there's any way we could know one way or the other."

"I don't think it's going to."

"Well, stop thinking then."

I looked up, surprised by the hard edge to her voice.

"People are responding well to the flyers. They're reading them and spreading the word. And the wanted posters have people talking even more. I've even heard people talking about Christianity."

I could imagine how excited Dad would be to hear about that. He'd find everything, even execution, worth it if people got saved.

"One way or another, you'll see him again," Ansley said.

"I don't want to wait till Heaven." I tightened my grip on the wheelchair handles. "Is that selfish of me?"

"I don't know. I guess it might be."

I smirked. Trust Ansley to give the straight answer. Maybe I needed to hear it. But needing to hear something didn't make it any more pleasant.

"You never know," Ansley continued, "maybe your dad will get out. The government hasn't dealt with anything like this in years. Who knows how they'll react?"

I forced a weak smile. "Have I ever mentioned that I like things planned out and contingencies allowed for?"

"Not sure if you've ever said it, but your dad and Bryce sure have."

I smiled a little.

"You can't deny that God's looking out for us." Ansley said after a few minutes. "So far no one's been arrested distributing posters. And Miss Lucy should have gotten killed or arrested today."

"I'm so glad she's alive."

"God sent a bit of encouragement just for you."

I smiled a little, unable to deny the fact. Unable to deny it until I heard the rhythmic pounding of running feet for the second time that day.

Chapter Thirteen

"Stay calm." Ansley squeezed my arm as we turned to see who was coming. "Maybe it's good news this time."

After all the commotion with Miss Lucy, I doubted a messenger would expend energy running except for urgent news. Urgent news was always bad news.

A boy ran up, panting. He looked familiar. I groped around in my memory, trying to land on the right name. Dirk? Derek? Damon? He didn't wait long enough for me to decide.

"Where's Bryce?" he asked.

"With Miss Lucy," Ansley said. "They're meeting us at my house. Why? What's wrong?"

"They're looking for him."

"They put out posters?" If something from the warehouse had factored into the raid, it was only a matter of time, but the news still hit like a punch.

The boy shook his head. "Nah. It seems like they don't want it so public this time. One of the spies saw it on the database. Had a school picture of him and everything."

I grimaced.

"A school picture?" Ansley frowned. "I thought Bryce went to a private school."

"His dad is the governor. They've got access to his school picture." I leaned on the wheelchair, then jumped when the front wheels popped off the ground.

"Here, let me take that." Ansley reached for the chair.

I surrendered it to her, trying to decide if I could find Bryce faster by backtracking and trying to catch up to him or meeting him at Ansley's house as we planned.

"Did the database say anything else?"

He nodded. "They've got The Agency on the case."

The Agency. I would love to write a flyer about The Agency. Normal citizens would be shocked to learn about the reign of terror their trusted government inflicted on Christians. They all enjoyed their blissful illusion of freedom.

I turned to the boy whose name I still couldn't remember. "Can you stay with Ansley and help her with the chair?"

"I guess so..." he hesitated. "Why?"

"I'm going the other way to see if I can catch up with him. You two keep going this way. That way one of us will reach him as soon as possible."

"Just be careful." Ansley frowned. Worry wrinkles creased her forehead. "Don't forget they're looking for you too."

"I will. You be careful too." I started jogging away from them, building up speed as I reached the corner and turned back towards Miss Lucy's apartment.

God, we prayed that You'd show us what You wanted us to do, and this seemed to be it. Please bless our work.

The verse that came to mind made my chest tighten. *For my thoughts are not your thoughts, neither are your ways my ways.*

I pushed myself to run faster. Sometimes it felt like I could outrun my problems for a few minutes. They always caught up, but sometimes they fell behind just for a moment.

I wanted God's thoughts and ways to match mine this time. I wanted His plan to include keeping Dad alive and not letting Bryce get arrested. How could I keep going without either one of them?

It made me think of a quote Miss Lucy and Mom liked. It said something like, "Don't let your happiness depend on something you may lose." I remembered it because C.S. Lewis, the author who said it, had quite a few books on the banned list. I had reluctantly added several of them to the incineration pile at the sorting center.

My lungs started to burn, and I forced myself to slow down. My legs felt like jello.

Two uniformed police officers crossed the intersection in front of me. I ducked between two buildings, heart pounding.

They kept going, and I breathed a sigh of relief.

When I started running again, I dashed across the intersection, just in case more police followed the original two.

By the time I reached Ansley's house, my legs felt ready to buckle. I'd seen no sign of Bryce or Miss Lucy, so I prayed they'd reached the house safely.

Ansley's mother, Mrs. Green, opened the door before I could knock.

"Good grief, you're red as a tomato, Heather. Come in. Quickly."

I stepped through the door and waited while she closed it. "Did Bryce and Miss Lucy get here?"

"A messenger brought Miss Lucy."

My legs gave out. I collapsed onto the storage bench by the door. "What happened to Bryce?"

"We don't think he got caught." She sat down next to me and rubbed my arm. "The messenger found him and warned him, so he took a different route to keep them away from Miss Lucy."

"Which route?" I clambered to my feet.

Mrs. Green grabbed my shoulder and pulled me back onto the bench. "You're not going anywhere. Stay still and stop fussing. I don't know which route."

"Thank God you're here." Ansley hurried down the hall. "I was worried sick when I found Miss Lucy here without you."

"I know the feeling."

"Come on." She grabbed my hand and pulled me up. "Let's go get you something to drink."

I followed her to the kitchen.

"Dad's working on straightening the dents out of Miss Lucy's chair. And we've got the tracts and press and flyers safe and sound in our hiding spot."

"That's good." I accepted the glass of water she held out and took a long gulp. I couldn't imagine Mr. Green, who always wore perfectly pressed suits, repairing anything.

"There's every reason to think Bryce will get away from them you know."

I pressed my lips together. "What makes you think that?"

"The messenger said they were still in the slums. I guarantee Bryce knows that area better than the police do. And there are plenty of places to hide or lose them."

"Bryce isn't the fastest runner."

She shrugged. "Neither are the police."

"Most police anyway." I set the empty glass down on the counter. "They've got the Agency assigned to his case. It's probably not ordinary cops chasing him."

"Fine, then. Assume they caught him and be miserable." She turned her back to me and dunked my cup into the dish water.

I grabbed the dish towel and stood next to her. When she rinsed the cup, I took it and dried it. "Sorry. I don't mean to sound so gloomy."

"I know." She smiled her forgiveness and headed for the living room. "Come on. Miss Lucy and Carmen are waiting."

Carmen. I'd forgotten she would be here. I followed Ansley.

Miss Lucy looked up and smiled at me as we walked in.

I sat down next to her on the couch and leaned into her hug.

"You okay?" Miss Lucy patted my leg.

I leaned back against the couch, forcing my body to relax. "Yeah. A little out of shape, that's all."

"Not to mention she probably sprinted the whole way here," Ansley added.

Carmen sat in an armchair. A coffee table separated the couch and chair. In her characteristic manner, she leaned forward to close the gap. "They're starting to get concerned about the posters."

"Of course they are. Their power is being threatened. By a sixteen-year-old girl no less." Miss Lucy gave a wry smile. "I can't imagine that makes certain government officials look very good."

She meant Governor Williams. Other government officials wouldn't be happy either, but he was our focus. He was the man with the power to waive Dad's sentence in order to keep any unrest from growing.

"So what do we do now?" I said. "It's good that they're paying attention and getting nervous, but we can't keep skittering around with our posters if they're focused on nabbing us."

"You'll need to modify your plan of attack slightly," Carmen said.

I traced the flower pattern on the couch cushion with my finger. What had made us think we could do this? Compared to the government...

I caught myself. What was I comparing? Me against the government looked as hopeless as it felt. But God against the government put a different spin on the picture.

"They're not exactly waiting on random street corners right now," Carmen continued. "If they were playing cat and mouse, it would have taken longer for them to find Miss Lucy's house in the slums. They had help."

I looked up and made eye contact with her. "The spy. I'm pretty sure it was a kid from the slums. Alden. He was at Miss Lucy's house with the police, and he's been watching us."

Carmen nodded. "I already put out a warning about him."

"How did they find out about Bryce?" If he got caught, it would be my fault. Not only because he was caught up in this because of me, but because my stupidity had allowed the government to take that picture of us.

"The grass," Carmen said.

I stared at her. Was I supposed to understand what that meant? Because I didn't.

"The grass at the warehouse," she continued. "Did it seem...?" She made a circular motion with her hand. I leaned forward. If I could guess what word she was looking for, I would help. "Did it seem unusual?" she finished.

Did it? I tried to remember. "Maybe?" Something tickled the back of my mind. Just out of reach.

"Maybe more synthetic?" she prompted.

"No." Now I remembered. "No. It seemed dead. I wondered why they didn't replace it with synthetic stuff that looked better."

"It *was* synthetic." Carmen flicked her private pocket screen on and turned it towards me. A confidential page from the government database filled the screen. It was an article about experimental grass.

"It's basically bug grass." Carmen flipped the screen around so she could look at it. "It's like being in a bugged room, but the grass itself is the microphone. They make it in the normal green color too, but they thought a dead grass look would make people assume it was natural."

"Worked on us." What had we talked about outside? My brain refused to produce a memory of our conversation.

"I don't know what exactly you guys said. But they did a search of all the warehouses when you started distributing the flyers. They found the recording of you at that warehouse, and that led to Bryce's signature on the books."

Bryce's signature. He was out there somewhere, hunted by the Agency. What would happen if they caught him? Would his father show mercy because Bryce was his son? Or would he use Bryce to prove his impartiality?

I rubbed my temples.

"I do believe we've got an answer to prayer." Carmen straightened.

"An answer to..." I raised an eyebrow.

"Listen." She held up a finger to silence me.

I obeyed and heard the front door click shut.

Ansley and I bounded out of our chairs in unison. We raced though the kitchen and down the hall to find Bryce, red-faced and panting, leaning against the door.

"Sorry I didn't knock." He offered a tired smile.

"I thought for sure they'd caught you." I flung my arms around him. Tears pricked the backs of my eyes. *Thank you. Thank you, God.*

He hugged back, smiling a little. "They didn't. They're probably still trying to get un-lost."

"I told her you'd make it." Ansley leaned against the wall and grinned at both of us. "She still worried herself half to death, though."

"You don't listen very well." Bryce tugged my braid. "You're worse than my mother."

That wasn't saying much. His mother didn't worry about him even when he disappeared overnight without telling either parent.

"You're still teasing." I pulled back to study him. "That's a good sign."

"I'm fine. Just tuckered." He sat down on the storage bench and yanked his left shoe off. A small pebble dropped into his palm. He pinched it between his thumb and index finger and held it up. "This thing has been a thorn in the flesh for about an hour."

"Poor you." I giggled, then slapped a hand over my mouth. "Sorry. It's not funny."

"Apparently it is."

"No." I shook my head. "I'm just so relieved."

"I know."

"I didn't think anyone could get redder than Heather was a few minutes ago," Ansley said. "But I think you take the prize, Bryce."

He pulled the hem of his shirt up to wipe his forehead. "I guarantee I'm sweating more."

"Come on." She pulled him up. "I'll get you a glass of water, too."

Bryce followed her but didn't waste time rehydrating. He chugged the water and bee-lined for the living room.

Miss Lucy grinned when she saw him. "We're going to have to call you Elijah."

"Why's that?" Bryce sat down next to her and gave her a hug.

"Elijah ran before Ahab's chariot to the entrance of Jezreel." She pulled back and kissed his cheek. "You just ran before the police pretty successfully."

"I guess so." He chuckled.

"You need to stay inside." I perched on the armrest of the couch. There was an empty chair across the room, but I wanted to be close to them. "At least for a few days."

"You wouldn't listen to me about that," he protested. "What makes you think...?"

"I listened for at least one full day," I interrupted. "And you're going to do the same."

He scowled at me.

"Actually, you're going to do more than that. But we'll argue about it later."

"What if I want to argue now?"

I shook my head. "No time for arguing. We need to figure out what to do next.

Bryce sobered. "You're right. Actually..." he looked at Carmen. "Can I have your pocket screen?"

Carmen turned it back on and passed it over.

No one else spoke as he flipped through the public database. His frown made conversation seem misplaced. The robotic click of the Greens' old grandmother clock filled the room.

"What are you looking for?" I kept my voice low and felt silly for doing so a second after the words left my mouth. There was no reason to keep quiet.

Bryce shook his head. He didn't look up.

"Bryce?"

"Heather, shush." He still didn't look at me.

The recently conquered fear snaked back into my stomach. "You're avoiding me. Why are you avoiding me?"

"I'm not..." Bryce trailed off and shrugged. He took a long swig of his water. "It's about your dad."

"What about him?" I forced the question out, but I didn't know if I wanted the answer. *Please, God, don't let him be dead. Please.*

Miss Lucy reached for my hand.

"He's okay. For now," Bryce said. He finally made eye contact. "They added him to the Recanting List."

The words settled like a kick in the stomach. It didn't surprise me. They couldn't deal with Dad quietly. He was too well known. People wanted to know what was going on, especially with speculation about the flyers swirling around like mad. The government had to make some sort of response.

When the government had to go public with a Christian arrest, they hid behind The Recanting List. The system forced the Christian to renounce his faith within a certain number of days or face execution. The government passed it off as fair because their victim controlled his own fate. So far, no one had questioned their reasoning.

"How long?" The words came out breathless, as if I was gasping for air after a long run.

"A week." Sympathy filled Bryce's expression.

I hugged myself and blinked back tears. Tears of grief instead of relief this time. One week. Dad had one week to renounce his faith or die.

Chapter Fourteen

I knelt in the Greens' guest bedroom and rested my forehead against the bed. I couldn't focus on praying. I couldn't focus on anything. My thoughts swirled into a tangle of what-ifs and memories.

Think, Heather, I scolded myself. I needed to get my mind in order, even if my emotions refused to be conquered.

Mom would scold me for that thought. She said the idea of uncontrollable emotions was another trick of the devil. She always seemed to have pretty good control of hers, but I hadn't mastered that yet. No surprise. I hadn't mastered most of the things Mom excelled at.

I forced my thoughts away from Mom. Thinking about her wouldn't help me come to a conclusion about my current problems. It just made me feel guilty, and I couldn't handle more guilt right now.

Bryce, Ansley and Miss Lucy were waiting downstairs. They said I could have as much time as I needed, but I knew they wanted to get to work on our next plan of attack. They had asked me to bring some of my favorite poems back with me Something about including one in a new flyer. I wasn't sure I liked that idea.

I fished around in my bag. My journal nested underneath the crumpled clothing. I pulled it out and started flipping through it.

The pages of poetry I normally found comforting made me cry till I couldn't read the words. I flipped to the back page of the journal and slid out the family photo. All of us looked so happy. I had been so little, so oblivious to everything dangerous. I traced my finger around our faces and warned myself not to drip any tears onto the picture.

I don't want Dad to die. I prayed. *Please, don't take him too. Not so soon. Not like this.*

The verse about God's way being different from men's wouldn't leave me. Why couldn't I get stuck on a better idea? I would rather think about God working everything together for good or hiding His people under his wings.

I don't want to lose him, I reiterated. As if maybe God hadn't gotten the point the first time.

I considered pulling Dad's Bible out, but fear stopped me. If God had a reason for sticking that frightening verse in my head, I didn't want the point emphasized.

I tucked the journal under my arm and headed downstairs.

Bryce and Miss Lucy looked up when I came in. Ansley shifted on the couch to make space for me between her and Miss Lucy.

I took the offered seat. "Where's Carmen?"

"She had to leave," Miss Lucy said.

"She said we've been doing a good job with the posters already so we probably didn't need her help," Bryce added.

"Who said anything about more posters?" I tucked my journal under my leg. It didn't surprise me that they wanted to do more, but I wasn't sure I wanted to go there.

"We have to," Ansley said.

"Why?"

"Because," Bryce made a sweeping gesture with his hand as if the reason was obvious, "we've got something going. We've got the police knocked off balance. And my dad must be at least a little surprised and confused after finding out about me."

I tried not to wince at his matter-of-fact tone. He made me feel selfish. I was drawing everyone into my fear of losing Dad. Bryce was brushing off the gravity of losing his own.

"Why does all that mean we need to make more posters?" I asked.

"We can't give them time to catch their balance. We can't give them a chance to regroup."

"It's working to make people talk," Ansley said. "Messengers are bringing in new reports all the time. That's why the government made the recanting announcement we think. So many people are asking questions."

"You really think your dad will do anything differently if people get upset about it?" I looked at Bryce. I hated to keep his dad in the conversation, but we needed to know.

He shrugged. "It's definitely possible. His job is to keep the people in this region from causing trouble. He won't want to risk his job over one execution."

I weighed my options. They were right. If we stopped distributing posters, the questions wouldn't last long. People would lapse back into blind belief of the government's explanations. But continuing our efforts put everyone in danger. Even greater danger now.

"People are reacting to your story," Miss Lucy said. "They care about the girl who's lost her dad."

Ansley nodded in agreement. "I think they're starting to love him as more than a live cast host because your love for him is so obvious in those flyers."

If I could somehow make them love Dad the way I loved him, Governor Williams wouldn't stand a chance. I almost managed a smile at the thought. We were a long way from that, but the idea was still encouraging.

"Did you bring your poems?" Ansley asked. "Can we put one of them in the flyer?"

"I don't write the kind of poetry people like to read."

"I like them," Bryce protested. "I'm a people."

"You know what I mean."

Bryce reached across the coffee table and squeezed my wrist. "Your poems are your heart. They're beautiful."

I felt my cheeks heat. Awkward.

He was right, though. My poems were my heart. I wasn't sure I wanted to lay my heart out for so many people to read.

They all looked at me expectantly.

"You want new text and a poem?" I asked.

Miss Lucy nodded. "Something personal. Something that will engage their emotions, not just their minds."

I took a deep breath. If it would help Dad, how could I refuse?

Take my heart, Lord make it thine,
Make it mold to Thy design.
Fill my mind with thoughts divine,
Let me rest in faith sublime.

All around the storm does rage,
Battles holy round me wage.
Satan whispers he has won,
Tempting me to turn and run.

Darkness fills the world around,
Keeping sinners firmly bound.
All alone my candle shines,
Let it to Thy will align.

Fill my quailing soul with might
Help me always do what's right
Never yielding to the night,
Pressing on with radiant light.

It hadn't taken long to reassemble the printing press in the Green's basement. The set up was less than ideal. I felt vulnerable printing forbidden material in a non-secret location. But it was the best we could do.

It also felt strange to see the words of one of my poems in print. I blushed when Ansley and Bryce took turns reading and complimenting it.

I snatched the paper away from Bryce as he began reading it out loud. "Cut it out."

He chuckled. "What's the matter?"

"It's bad enough strangers are going to be reading it. I don't want to listen to how bad it sounds right before it gets distributed."

"But it sounds great!" Ansley protested.

I scowled at her, and she grinned back.

I shook my head as she trotted off to show her parents.

"What happens if all this works?" I addressed the question to Miss Lucy.

"What do you mean?"

"If people read our flyers. If they decide they've got an issue with what's going on. If they start bugging Governor Williams about how he's handling this."

"We gain momentum." She took one of the flyers off the coffee table and scanned it. "Momentum and size if all goes well. You know how it works. The more support we get, the better chance we have of forcing the government to listen to us."

I shook my head. "What if they decide they're not going to listen? What if they decide to live up to what they're supposed to be? Fascist countries don't listen to the people. I don't want to cause more arrests."

"Even in a conquering army..." Miss Lucy began.

"There are casualties," I finished. "I know all about that. But the idea here is to get Dad out of prison, not get more people arrested."

"Is that the real reason?" She raised her eyebrows.

"No. The real reason is to do what God wants me to." I parroted the right answer. The one she expected to hear. I wanted it to be true, but I struggled to keep it as my main focus. "That doesn't change the fact that I still don't want more people to get hurt."

Miss Lucy gave me a look that made me think she could read my thoughts. She shifted back in the couch. "Did you ever hear about Sergeant York?"

"No." I shook my head.

"Alvin York got drafted during the First World War. He tried to get out of fighting. He didn't want to kill anyone."

I nodded. So we had something in common, Sergeant York and I. Except I didn't have to do any killing with my own hands. Instead my actions could lead others to death.

"What happened?" I asked.

"He had to go to war anyway. During the battle he realized he could save more lives by taking out key enemy positions than he could by doing nothing."

I chewed my lip. That made sense. Sort of. If some government leaders got knocked out of position, persecution might decrease. I doubted I would ever have the power to do that, though.

"Sergeant York preserved as many enemy lives as he possibly could alongside the lives of his own men and allies."

"But there were still some casualties."

"Yes. There were still some casualties."

161

"I hear you." I sighed. "But I don't think I could take out any 'key positions' even if I tried to."

"There's a major difference in this situation," she said. "We're still talking physical casualties, but there's potential to rescue spiritual lives."

"That doesn't make me feel much better about the physical casualties." I wondered if Mr. and Mrs. Green would feel good about potential spiritual advances if Ansley died. They were better Christians than me if they would.

"Matthew 10:28," Bryce said.

I thought for a second before remembering the verse. "Fear not them which kill the body, but are not able to kill the soul: but rather fear him which is able to destroy both soul and body in hell." One of those verses that sounded beautiful and poetic but got hard the second you faced the reality of it.

They watched me, waiting for my reaction. I felt like throwing something.

"It's too much for me," I said after a while. "And please don't tell me that if it's too much for me, I need to trust God. Because I'm trying."

More silence. Great. I'd scared them away from saying anything.

I bit my lip and turned to Miss Lucy. "I'm sorry. I'm just scared. I don't want Dad to die, and I'm scared." There. I'd said it out loud.

"I know." She pulled me into a hug. "It's okay."

It wasn't okay, but I didn't argue. Her arms around me helped steady my inner turmoil. I closed my eyes and put my head on her shoulder.

"Maybe God intended Ray's arrest to be the catalyst for change." She kept her voice firm and steady, but her arms tightened around me. "Change in your heart. Change in ours. Maybe change in the whole country." She smiled. "Ray would consider it worth it."

Chapter Fifteen

The Greens made me and Bryce stay home and work on production instead of helping distribute the next batch of flyers. Ansley came home with story after story of people's reactions.

The head of police made several announcements declaring that he and the governor were in conversation about shutting down the religious propagandist. Citizens of both the main city and outlying areas were warned not to accept or believe our posters. They took them anyway, and the buzz grew.

"Still no public announcement about me. Dad's trying to save face." Bryce examined my picture plastered onto a new wanted poster. The government was cranking out flyers at a ridiculous speed, but they weren't having as much success with their campaign.

"Your mom must be worried sick." I almost felt bad for her.

"She'll fret, not worry. There's a difference." He rolled the poster up and flashed an, it's-no-big-deal smirk. Liar. "I'm sure she has enough entertaining to keep her distracted. I swear if she could host ten tea parties a day, she would."

I couldn't imagine a mom who could be distracted by tea parties when her son was in danger.

"Everyone is talking about you." Ansley came up behind us and grabbed the poster from Bryce. She waved it at me. "It's like you're a celebrity or something."

"I don't want to be a celebrity." Most celebrities seemed vapid and self-important. That wasn't the impression I hoped to create. "We need this to be more than a fad."

"That part is up to you." Miss Lucy pressed her ink-smudged fingertips together.

"I don't know what to do that won't either get me killed or seem like a stupid publicity stunt." We needed something beyond posters to encourage people to choose a side. In order for all of this to benefit Dad, they needed to move beyond talking among themselves. They needed to make the government aware of their concern.

"We need to keep everything genuine." Bryce nodded as if agreeing with himself. "Raw and real and emotional."

"That sounds scary." I didn't know how long I could keep exposing raw emotion. It hurt too much. But losing Dad would hurt more. Way more.

"We need to figure out our next step." Ansley smoothed a wanted poster and flipped it to the blank side. "Any ideas?"

Silence. I tipped back in my chair and slid into a slouch. We were running out of steam.

Mr. Green walked into the room. He hesitated when he saw us.

"What's up, Dad?" Ansley waved her pen at him. "Any ideas for the next phase of this thing?"

Mr. Green smiled. A forced smile if I ever saw one. "Sorry. No." He turned to me. "Heather. I need to talk to you."

"Um. Okay." I stood up. His expression didn't make me eager to follow him. Did I do something wrong? Was he upset at me for putting Ansley in danger? I wouldn't blame him, but why would he invite me to stay here if he didn't want her involved?

"There's something you need to see." He headed down the hall and gestured for me to follow.

"What happened? Did I do something?" I half-jogged to catch up. No matter what he wanted to show me, it wasn't good news. Nothing about Mr. Green's expression and posture left room for good news.

"I'd rather let you see for yourself," he said.

My mind raced through possibilities as I followed him through the house. Bryce was okay. We knew he was being searched for, but he hadn't left the house. It had only been two days since the news about Dad. Had they changed their mind about something?

"Is it Dad?" I stopped in the hall, legs trembling. "I don't want to get bad news off the screen."

"He's still alive, honey." Mr. Green guided me into his home office and closed the door behind us. The screen on his desk flickered, a little icon popping up, then fading. Dad called the lightshow a screensaver; a left over from old computers.

As a lawyer, Mr. Green had access to public and semi-private databases. Ansley said it cost so much money he'd avoided buying the access at first, but his wealthier clients expected him to have it.

"What is it?" I hung back, still afraid to look.

He wiggled the mouse and the screen returned to a familiar database. It was the government announcement page that the school and sorting center screens went to automatically.

I forced myself to walk forward and look at the screen. A chill gripped me before I could even begin to read. A picture of Dad, obviously taken at the prison, filled the upper left-hand side of the screen.

"What happened?" I repeated.

Mr. Green shook his head. A muscle in his cheek twitched. He wasn't going to tell me. He was like that. He liked to let people learn the facts for themselves. I often appreciated that side of his character, but right now I longed for a gentler approach.

I turned back to the screen and scanned the words. After a few seconds, I realized that I wasn't processing any of them. The words were coming into my head and bouncing right back out. I took a deep breath and started over.

The headline read "Recanting Meeting Rescheduled."

For a second, I felt a surge of hope. Perhaps I'd misinterpreted Mr. Green's expression. Maybe he wasn't telling me because it was *good* news. Perhaps...

The next line dashed my momentary hopes.

"May 9th." Two days. In less than 48 hours, Dad would die.

Chapter Sixteen

The sobs came so hard and strong, I knew I couldn't stop them. I crumpled onto the desk chair and covered my face.

Mr. Green rubbed my back as I cried.

Two days. Hopeless. How could I change in two days what better people in the generation before mine hadn't been able to change in their lifetime? *God, please.*

God please what? Was it okay to beg Him for Dad's life? Was I supposed to sacrifice Dad willingly like Abraham with Isaac? Maybe God would save him at the last minute like He did for Isaac. Dad wasn't a special, promised heir, though.

Bryce tapped on the door and poked his head in. "What's wrong? What happened?"

"It's Dad." I swiped at my eyes. They burned from crying so much.

"What about him?" Bryce stepped into the room. The color drained out of his face.

"They've moved the date of the Recanting Meeting. We only have two days."

Bryce started to swear but cut himself off. He leaned over to scan the announcement. "It doesn't make sense. People are already agitated about the possibility of him getting executed. This is going to set them off worse."

"That's probably the reason," Mr. Green said. "He's getting too much sympathy. The governor is trying to cut this off before it gains too much momentum."

My fault. Again. If I hadn't gotten everyone talking, they wouldn't be so focused on getting Dad out of the way.

"Won't this just get him more sympathy?" Bryce asked.

Mr. Green shrugged. "They're taking a calculated risk."

I pulled my hair back and held it off my neck. "A girl trying to save her father's life is more sensational than a girl mourning her father's death."

The angry muscle in Bryce's jaw pulsed.

I focused on slowing my heart rate and filling my lungs. Passing out wouldn't help anyone or anything. "I need some time to think."

"Yeah." Bryce pushed his fingers through his hair and scratched his scalp. "I bet we all do."

I stood up. My vision darkened, and I put a hand on the desk to steady myself.

"Whoa." Bryce jumped towards me. "Careful."

"Just a little dizzy. It's gone." I managed a straight line to the door. "Ask everyone to pray."

Miss Lucy leaned forward in her repaired wheelchair and raised her eyebrows at me. "What's this about?"

I looked around the living room and made eye contact with everyone. Miss Lucy first, then Bryce and Ansley.

"We were talking about a plan earlier. Before the news." I worked to keep my voice steady. I needed to keep it together and sound confident. "We still need one."

We needed one more than ever. And we needed one that would accelerate fast.

"You sound like you have something in mind," Ansley said.

"Maybe." My mind-blank from earlier was gone. Now that the dam had broken, thoughts and ideas were flooding my brain. Ideas that would work. The trick was communicating them without making everyone panic.

"People are talking plenty by now," I said. "We need to convert curiosity into support."

"So what are you proposing?" Miss Lucy asked.

"From what the messengers say, people are curious about me." Rumor had it that privately owned recordings of my screen appearances with Dad were selling for ridiculous prices on the black market. "They want to meet me."

Bryce snickered.

I scowled at him. "Celebrity is on the bottom of my desired careers list. Especially with the region's entire police force looking for me."

"We're agreed on that point anyway." He stopped laughing. "You need to lay low."

I rolled my eyes and reminded myself to tread carefully. I didn't want Bryce to know my full plan. Not yet anyway. Maybe not until I carried it out. "Anyway, since people want to talk to me, whether I like it or not, I thought we could use that to our advantage."

They all waited, so I continued.

"If I went to a public area and just started sharing my story, I bet a big crowd would gather pretty quickly."

"Please tell me I did not hear you say that." Bryce groaned. "That's ridiculous. The police will gather just as fast as the crowd."

"Police will need time to receive orders and get to the location." I knew how they operated. The government used whatever means necessary to repress religion, no matter how brutal. But government-trained law enforcement never did anything without orders. "I could share my story and our team could hand out flyers to the crowd. It would be easier to blend into a crowd."

"For the messengers, sure. But what about you?"

I shrugged. "People seem to like me. I think I could slip into the crowd and disappear long enough to get away."

"I don't like it," Bryce said. "I don't like it one bit. It's too risky. It doesn't make any sense for you to get yourself arrested because you're making a foolhardy attempt to rescue your father."

"It's not foolhardy," I snapped. "Risky, yes. But not foolhardy. It could work."

In truth, I had no intention of slipping into the crowd. Hearing me talk didn't carry enough impact to change lifetimes of complacency. As usual, Bryce was right. If my only goal was talking to people, a live appearance was too risky. I had more in mind.

"Tell her not to do it," Bryce addressed his plea to Miss Lucy. "Make her remember she doesn't like taking risks."

"I'm not sure what I think yet," Miss Lucy said. "And I reserve judgment until I have more time to think it over."

Bryce and I glanced at each other. He'd explode if he knew the rest of my plan. I needed to talk to Miss Lucy alone.

"As for reminding her she's not a risk taker," Miss Lucy continued. "She wasn't always cautious, Bryce. And even if she was, people grow."

He frowned.

"Not the reaction he was looking for," Ansley said.

"I know." Miss Lucy smiled. "Unless you young folks have more to discuss, I'd like to go pray."

"I can take you to your room." Ansley stood up and reached for the wheelchair handles. Miss Lucy could take herself, but the Greens' carpeted floors were challenging for her.

Bryce watched them leave. "I still don't like it."

"Neither do I," I admitted, "but it makes sense."

"It does not!"

I groaned. "Let's not start that again." Arguing was hard when I agreed with him. My plan made more sense when the second part was added. It would be too much for Bryce to handle, though.

"But, Heather..."

"Just pray about it, okay?" I waved my hand for him to hush. "We'll see what Miss Lucy thinks."

I could see by his expression that he didn't like my answer, but he gave in.

"Okay, I'll pray."

"Pray that we'll find God's will, not yours."

He grimaced. "I'll pray, okay?"

I sighed and gave him a quick side hug. I kept running my plan through my mind over and over again, searching for holes and finding plenty. Risk paved every potential road to getting enough sympathy to force the governor to choose mercy. I needed to talk to Miss Lucy.

"I can't tell if we're winning or losing, Bryce," I said. "Maybe we're doing both."

"What do you mean?"

"People are talking. They're thinking about Christians. Learning about Christians. Hearing about God. Questioning the government. That's good."

He crossed his ankle across the opposite knee and nodded. His foot jiggled. The nervous energy in the motion put me on edge.

"But I'm not sure if we're any closer to helping Dad." I forced myself to focus on Bryce's face instead of his foot. "No matter what I'm doing, I can feel the time running out for him."

"We'll give it our best shot." He wrapped an arm around my shoulders and squeezed. "I know it's not much, but..."

"It's enough." I forced a smile. "Has anyone handed out flyers in the main city?"

I said it in my most innocent voice, but Bryce still frowned.

"Yeah," he said. "Why?"

"Where in the city?"

"One of the greens. I don't know which one." He shifted to stare at me. "Not that it should make a difference to you. I thought you'd never been to the main city."

"I haven't." The sorting center was only a short walk away from the main city border, but I'd never felt the need to explore outside of my normal sphere of activity.

"I don't like the way your brain is working."

I ignored him. "How many flyers?"

"How should I know?" He voice cracked in an indignant squeak.

"Maybe Ansley will." I shrugged. The city was the most logical place to try to draw a crowd. "With all the gossip going around, I have a feeling people in the city know what's going on."

"Why does it matter?" Bryce grabbed my shoulder. "Heather, please, don't make any rash decisions."

"I'm not being rash about anything. I'm not a rash person."

He snorted. "I used to believe that. What are you planning?"

"I already told you."

"Yeah. Draw a big crowd, talk to them all, and then use them as cover to escape from the police."

"Bryce, I asked you to just pray about it. I'll make my final decision after I talk to Miss Lucy."

"You're not listening to me." Bryce scowled. "You're trying to talk me out of it."

"Of course I'm trying to talk you out of it!" Bryce squeaked again. "I told your Dad I'd try to take care of you."

"Bryce." I made eye contact. "I never thought I'd do any of the things I've done over the past few days. I can't quit now."

"But what if..."

"No. Please." I held my hand up. "I really believe this is what God wants me to do, Bryce."

"What if it isn't?"

"If Miss Lucy says no, I won't do it. Promise." I chewed my lip. Could I really stand by and watch Dad die? I glanced at Bryce and my chest tightened. Could I risk my best friend's life by pulling him into this crazy plan?

"Are you okay?" Bryce touched my shoulder.

"Bryce, please, just trust me. I need you on my team."

"I'm on your team." He squeezed my hand. "And I'm on your Dad's team too. Honest."

"I know."

"It just scares me when you don't listen."

"Wisdom in a multitude of counselors," I said quietly. A lesson hard learned and easily forgotten, at least for me. "Don't worry, I haven't forgotten. It's just that your counsel is too emotional."

He scowled at me.

"That's exactly what I'm talking about." I indicated his expression.

"I don't want to see you die too." He wore an expression too serious to brush off.

"I know." I gave him another hug. "Thank you."

Dying was the least of my concerns. Interrogation scared me more. The thought of getting Bryce hurt or killed scared me the most. I couldn't let anything happen to him.

Two days. My thoughts ran wild as I walked down the hall. Could I really do anything about Dad in that much time? Of course, it didn't even take one day for David to defeat Goliath. But Goliath was only one man, and I didn't have the army of Israel at my back. Unless you counted the underground church.

No matter which way I looked at it, I kept remembering how few of my plans met with success. So far the posters were working well, but how long would my luck hold out?

I tried to think of other miracles that might relate to Dad's situation.

Paul. Paul got stoned by people who were mad about his faith. They left him for dead and he got right back up. I could go for that kind of result.

On the other hand, Stephen got stoned too, and he didn't get back up. And Paul eventually got beheaded.

I sighed. At least David died of old age.

The door to the guest bedroom was open. Miss Lucy sat at a small desk, sketching on a piece of recycled paper.

I tapped on the doorframe. "Can I come in?"

"Of course, child." She turned and smiled. "I hope you don't mind me wasting a piece of paper. My hands get itchy when I don't have a painting to work on."

"I don't mind." I sat down on the bed and rubbed my hands over my knees. "I'm sorry we had to leave most of your art stuff behind."

"Just a bunch of stuff." She waved a hand. "I've lost it all before, and if I live long enough, I'll probably lose it all again. Things come and go."

"Just like people."

"No. Not like people." She patted my hand. "People come and go here in this world, but we're eternal creatures. My paintings aren't."

We sat in silence for a few moments. Miss Lucy went back to shading her sketch. The familiar whisper of pencil against paper coaxed my raw nerves to relax.

"I'm scared, Miss Lucy. I want to be willing to lose him, but I'm scared."

"I know. I'd rather not lose him either." She set the pencil down. "Ray and I have been friends for a long, long time."

"I don't think we can stop it. There isn't enough time." I felt I might choke on the words. My unsteady voice betrayed the ever present threat of tears.

"You're right, we can't stop it."

I froze for a second, then realized what she meant. "I know God can, but that doesn't make me feel much better."

"It's okay to be frightened."

Even more comforting. To be fair, though, I wasn't sure anything could cheer me up right now. Anything short of Dad walking through the front door.

I forced a wry laugh. "Bryce might not be so worried about me making brash decisions if he saw me right now."

"And I have a feeling you might not find him as intent on talking you out of every possible risk if you saw him right now."

"What do you mean?" I frowned and raised an eyebrow.

"Bryce loves your father almost as much as you do." She patted my leg and gave my knee a quick squeeze. "He just shows his concern differently than you do."

I sighed.

Miss Lucy smiled and put her fingertips together. "Now. I'm guessing you have more up your sleeve. Something Bryce wouldn't approve of."

I gaped. "How did you know?"

"You brushed Bryce's concerns off too fast. Without a good enough reason. Plus I can just tell."

I hesitated. "Do you think Bryce could tell?"

She shook her head. "I don't think so. He would have called you on it."

I didn't think he suspected either, but the confirmation brought relief.

"So what's the rest of your plan?"

"I think we need to focus on distributing flyers in the main city. Where there's a higher concentration of people."

She nodded. "That's logical. Bryce shouldn't find it too disturbing."

"No," I agreed. "I actually mentioned the city to him. It's the second part I don't want him to know about. I don't want him to know even if I end up doing it."

Her forehead wrinkled. "Let's hear it."

"I think we should hand out as many flyers as possible in the next two days. Hopefully people will continue to respond positively to them."

She nodded.

I took a deep breath. "We only have two days. People are going to need some drastic motivation to put pressure on the governor in that much time."

I paused. The next part of the plan was frightening even in theory. I didn't want to do it. But I didn't see any other way.

"What are you getting at, Heather?" Miss Lucy picked up the pencil and twirled it between her fingers. "What's the conclusion?"

"I want to talk to a crowd of people."

She nodded patiently. "You already mentioned that."

"I know." I took another deep breath. "But I don't want to run away when the police show up."

If I were arrested in front of a crowd of sympathetic spectators, the stories in our posters would become real to them. The people would be exposed to what they couldn't adequately imagine without experiencing it for themselves. If they reacted the way I hoped they would, my arrest would fan sparks into flames.

Miss Lucy's face remained neutral, almost emotionless. It stayed that way for a long time.

I waited, wishing I could see the thoughts going through her mind. Did she understand my reasoning, or did she think I was crazy?

The plan could fail. It probably would fail. But with all the work I'd put into stirring things up, it was only a matter of time before they arrested me anyway. If it happened now, it might fuel the outcry we needed.

I realized I was trying to force a scenario similar to the most famous Bible story of all. Pontius Pilate had allowed Jesus' death to pacify the people and preserve his position. Surely Governor Williams wasn't stronger than Pilate.

"You know you'll probably die," Miss Lucy said. "You and Ray both."

"If I don't do it, we'll both die anyway. It'll just take them a little longer to get me."

"It won't be easy. They know you're leading this whole effort. They'll try to get names and information out of you. It will put everyone at risk."

"What we're doing now puts everyone at risk. You said that even conquering armies have casualties."

"Actually, a guy called Brother Andrew said that originally. It is true, though." She tapped the pencil against the desk. "Have you prayed about it?"

I nodded.

"And you feel it's what God wants you to do?"

"I didn't ask for some miraculous sign or anything." I wasn't a fleece-before-the-Lord type. "But I feel more peaceful about the idea than I think I could on my own."

"You're sure it's peace and not numbness?"

I nodded. "I know the difference. I still feel sick to my stomach when I'm numb. That's what happened after they arrested Dad. This is different. It's not me. Like Bryce says, I'm not really a risk taker anymore."

Miss Lucy studied me. "Why is that, Heather? You used to want to take on the world."

"I was stupid." My words came too fast and too sharp. I sounded angry. "I mean. I'm sorry..."

"You were admired. We were all convinced God had great things in store for you."

"I don't want to be great." I looked away from her. All the adults' praises and dreams for me had made me think too much of myself. If I had thought more about caution and less about taking on the world, Mom might still be alive.

Mom's face flashed into my mind before I could stop it. Not the smiling face from my treasured photograph. No, this was an image burned into my mind. I had no picture of it, but I would never need one. I could remember the blank, glassy eyes with as much detail as if I had looked away from them moments before. I could still see the blood on her forehead in vivid detail.

"I think you need to face the past." Miss Lucy scooted her chair towards me and put a hand on my shoulder.

"No!" I jerked away from her.

"You can't carry through with what you're planning without making peace." She kept her voice low. I could feel her trying to make eye contact, but I refused to accept it.

"Yes, I can." If I let myself think more about the past, I'd be useless to everyone.

Had I said goodbye to Dad when he pushed the Bibles into my hands? I tried to remember, but the events of the night blurred. All I could remember was him shouting at me to go. The same way Mom had shouted.

I pushed the memories away, both the ones of Mom and of Dad. I couldn't go there now. Not now, not ever.

"You can't afford to doubt your plans now." Miss Lucy cupped her hand around my chin and forced me to look at her. She stared into my eyes. "As long as you blame yourself for what happened to your mother, you'll second guess what you're doing now."

"What happened to Mom *was* my fault!" Did everyone honestly think it wasn't? Mom printed Bibles and made deliveries, but her foolhardiness ended there. She followed protocol and had little to fear.

I clutched my head as the memories kept coming. Just as I always feared, they refused to stop once they got started.

"No." I moaned. "I can't, Miss Lucy. Please."

"Shh." She braced her arms on the bed and swung onto the mattress next to me.

"I can't do this," I said. "I can't remember."

She. wrapped her arms around me. "What happened wasn't your fault, Heather. You need to stop thinking that way."

The memories kept coming. The sound of the gun. That moment when the world felt muted because I could no longer hear Mom's footsteps. The return of sound a moment later as her body hit the pavement.

"It was my fault. It was all my fault."

Mom had told me to go, to keep running her rasping, blood-choked voice penetrating me like no other words I had ever heard.

"I should never have asked her to make that delivery." I ducked out of Miss Lucy's embrace and stood. Tension charged my body. I wanted to run, but I couldn't. I started to pace the room.

"She wanted to make it."

"No, she didn't. She said she had a bad feeling about it. I should have listened. I shouldn't have pushed." Mom was used to curbing my impetuosity. Why had she given in at the worst possible time?

"She felt like she should go," Miss Lucy said quietly. "She prayed about it and asked me and your father for advice. We all decided it was important to get those Bibles out before the distribution point closed."

I hesitated mid-step. "You did?" Why hadn't Dad told me?

"Yes, darling, we did." Miss Lucy pressed her lips into a half-smile. "We knew the police were suspicious about that point, but we had no other way of getting Bibles to the new church."

I nodded. My one comfort about Mom's death was the success of our mission. I remembered walking the alleys and hearing the occasional scuff of feet behind us. Each time the sound had been so faint we thought our strained senses were fabricating danger. With nothing solid to act on, we kept going. The police didn't jump us until after the Bibles changed hands. Unless they had found another provider, those were the last Bibles those Christians received.

"When you wanted to go so badly, your Mom felt God was telling her to conquer her fears."

"But why?" I sagged back onto the bed. "We shouldn't have gone."

"Don't ask me to explain God, child." Miss Lucy hugged me. "I only know that your mother's death was not your fault."

The words were a crack in the boulder of guilt that had burdened me for so long. As the weight began to crumble away, grief bubbled through the crack.

"Why did she have to die?" I blinked back tears. My head already throbbed from crying so much.

"I don't know." Miss Lucy pushed my hair out of my face. Her wrinkled hand felt soft and cool against my skin. "Maybe to prepare you and your father for this day."

"What if I fail?" I whispered. I hadn't been able to save Mom. I hadn't even said goodbye.

"Esther 4:14." Miss Lucy gave me a verse the way Bryce so often did. The words came to my mind as soon as she spoke the reference.

"Who knoweth whether thou art come to the kingdom for such a time as this," I whispered. It wasn't the full verse, but I knew Miss Lucy was referring to that part of it.

She smiled and squeezed my hand. "Perhaps you're our Esther."

"I don't think so." I could never compare to such a respected Bible figure. Even if Mom's death wasn't my fault, I was no deliverer.

"Esther was a scared, brave young woman. Just like you."

Just like me. I felt a tiny ray of hope. "So you think I should do it?"

Miss Lucy nodded. "I'll not be the one to stand in your way."

Chapter Seventeen

The next morning, I woke with a churning stomach. I went right to the bathroom and spent fifteen minutes splashing my face with cold water and hovering around the toilet.

After convincing myself I was simply playing physiological games, I left the bathroom and dressed in a knee-length black skirt and well-fitting blue t-shirt.

When I examined myself in the mirror, I knew I looked like people expected me to. Different from everyone else. My understated outfit was the antithesis of current trends. I felt comfortable. Like I was shedding the Goth girl I had been for so long and settling into my own skin.

Miss Lucy flashed me a knowing, sympathetic smile when I walked into the kitchen.

I poured myself a glass of juice and sat down at the kitchen table. When Bryce came in a few minutes later, the cup remained untouched.

"Nervous about tomorrow?" Bryce slid into the seat next to me.

"Do I look nervous?"

He shook his head. "Not really. You look sick."

"Bit of an upset stomach."

"What are you planning, Heather?" He toyed with his toast. It sprayed crumbs across the table. "I can't believe handing out flyers in the city is all you have in mind."

"Bryce, let's not have that conversation again. Not right now." I took a sip of my juice and hoped my stomach wouldn't revolt. I couldn't tell him. I had to protect him from the kind of guilt that had haunted me for so long.

He couldn't stop what he didn't know about. He couldn't assume responsibility forever. He would feel horrible for a while, but if I didn't tell him my plans, he would eventually realize that he had been powerless.

"There's still hope," Bryce said. "Anything could happen between now and tomorrow."

I nodded. "I know."

Daniel got sentenced to death. Like Dad, he refused to sacrifice his faith in exchange for his life. And he came out of the lions' den unscathed.

Shadrach, Meshach, and Abednego's story also bore distinct similarities to Dad's. They refused to bow down to the false god and were sentenced to death as a result. They got thrown into a fiery furnace and didn't even smell of smoke when they came out.

Miracles could still happen, right? We served the same God as Daniel, David, Shadrach, Meshach and

Abednego. We also served the same God Paul and Stephen did.

I'd rather have a Daniel story this time, Lord, if it's all the same to you. I swished my juice, watching it swirl against the edges of the glass.

"You're supposed to drink that, you know."

I glanced up and smirked at Bryce. "I know."

"Thought maybe you forgot. You're looking at it like it's some new art form or something."

"It's going to be a new art form on your shirt if you don't watch it." I tried to force a smile to make my words seem teasing instead of grouchy. Judging by the look on Bryce's face, my effort failed.

When I took another sip of the juice, my stomach stayed calm. The rest of the juice soon followed with equal success.

"At least my shirt's safe now," Bryce said as I took the last swallow.

"I wouldn't count on it." I got up and put the glass in the sink. "I know where to get more."

This time Bryce chuckled. He grabbed a bowl from the center of the table and pulled it towards him, then hesitated. "Do you want to leave now or do I have time for breakfast?"

"You have time for breakfast."

I left the room and went back upstairs to my bedroom. My bag leaned against the wall. I pushed the pillow against the headboard and sat down, pulling the bag onto my lap.

I took Dad's Bible and my journal out and hugged both to my chest. It made me feel silly and sentimental, but I couldn't help it. I could feel my heart beating against the cover of the Bible.

After a few moments, I put the Bible down and slid the photograph out of my journal. Tears sprang to my eyes as I studied the three smiling faces looking back at me.

God is my salvation; I will trust, and not be afraid: for the Lord Jehovah is my strength and my song; he also is become my salvation.

I put the picture on top of the Bible and flipped my journal to a blank page.

The poem flowed almost effortlessly onto the page. I couldn't believe I'd never written one based on my comfort verse before, but it fit to do one now. It pulled my jumbled thoughts together and sorted them out on the paper.

I will trust and not be afraid.
Upon God's salvation I'm staid.
Though thoughts of doubt may oft evade,
They cannot, will not, mind pervade.

For God above shall be my strength,
My song to sing in face of death,
With all His love's unmeasured breadth,
Though walking through the stormy depth.

"Heather?" Bryce hollered from the bottom of the stairs. "Ready when you are."

I read the lines of the poem again. Most of my poems were longer, but I didn't think I'd add to this one even if, by some miracle, I had opportunity to.

"Coming!" I called back.

I picked up the photo and put one finger against Dad's face. It felt like the ache in my chest might suffocate me.

"I love you, Daddy," I whispered. "I really do."

I tucked the photo back into my journal and slid both into my bag.

Bryce met me at the bottom of the stairs, a stack of flyers tucked under his arm.

"I feel like we're bringing newspapers back into existence," he said. "We're getting pretty good at production."

I took half of them from him and stuffed them into a borrowed messenger bag. The outside pages stuck to my clammy hands.

I will trust and not be afraid.

"You sure you're okay to do distribution today?" Bryce leaned over to examine my face. "You're awfully pale."

"Nervous about Dad, that's all." I hurried towards the door. I didn't want to argue about it. If Bryce managed to pry my plan out of me, it would make things so much harder.

He followed me out the door, snagging his bike— one borrowed from Ansley—from where it leaned against the porch. I could hear him fumbling to get onto it quickly.

I kept walking. He probably thought I was mad at him. I was sorry for that, but I didn't slow down.

It didn't take him long to catch up. When he drew even with me, he slowed, weaving back and forth to stay next to me.

"You know your dad isn't afraid to die," he said after a few minutes.

"Of course I know."

"Just checking." He lapsed back into silence.

"Bryce," I bit my lip and looked up at him, "I'm sorry. I don't mean to be so snappish."

"It's okay. I understand."

Bryce would be devastated when I got arrested. He would hate himself for not protecting me.

But it would make things worse if I told him, and he still failed to keep me safe. Worse still if he succeeded in keeping me out of harm's way. I had to do this.

"Ready to split up?" I glanced at Bryce as we stopped on a city street corner.

"Guess here works as good as anywhere." He wheeled his bike a few yards down a side street and locked it to a telephone pole. He took his flyers out of the bike pouch and walked back to me. "Promise you'll be careful?"

I hesitated. It all depended on how you defined careful.

Bryce narrowed his eyes. "Heather, what is going through that mind of yours?"

"Thoughts." I rolled onto my toes and planted a quick kiss on his cheek. "Don't worry about me so much. I'll be fine."

"That's not..."

"I said I'll be fine." I interrupted. "Now stop worrying."

"You're giving me every reason in the world to worry," he said, but he let it drop and gave me a quick hug. "I'm serious, Heather. I don't want anything to happen to you."

"I know you don't." I hugged him back. For one uncertain moment I wanted to tell him and let him protect me. I didn't want to let him go. But I did. "You be careful, too."

We headed down opposite roads. The instinctive way we tucked our stacks of flyers under our arms made me smile. It didn't take long to become accustomed to an activity, even an illegal one.

After Bryce disappeared from view, I found a quiet spot between two buildings and pulled out my pen. It took two hours for me to write "CENTER GREEN, 12 NOON" across the top of each flyer. Hopefully, people's curiosity would lure them to come without more information than the place and time. If everyone was trying to solve the mystery of what was happening on the Center Green at twelve noon, it would help word spread quickly.

I readjusted my wig and secured a baseball cap over it. I need to hand out all my flyers as fast as possible. If people recognized me, I'd never reach that goal.

I hurried to the main road, offering flyers to every person I walked past. Most of them accepted.

Our flyers enjoyed a degree of fame in and of themselves. Never since the paper rationing had anyone outside of the government been able to spread news to as many people as we had reached with our flyers.

Plenty of people wanted their own flyer just so they could say they had one. A few messengers reported people asking for extras to give to friends and family.

Their oblivion to danger never ceased to amaze me. They couldn't seem to grasp the government's capacity for cruelty. Perhaps my arrest in the afternoon would change that. Or perhaps people would try to forget about the whole situation in an effort to return to their comfortable, self-centered lives. I'd find out soon enough.

I shed my wig and arrived at the green at eleven-thirty. My plan had worked better than I dared to hope. People already blanketed the grassy field. They milled about and filled the area with the buzz of conversation. I tugged my ball cap lower, and leaned against the fence surrounding the green to watch a steady stream of people join the crowd.

If my flyers worked this fast, the people congregating here could be trusted to spread the word of my arrest even faster. By tonight, everyone would be talking about it.

A sudden doubt flashed through my mind. What if the government saw through my plan? What if they decided not to arrest me in front of everyone? They could have me followed and arrest me with less fuss on my way home.

No. I brushed the idea away. The Governor was getting frustrated. His warnings were being ignored.

Everything was coming out in the open. He had to show the citizens that he wouldn't tolerate religion.

"Heather?" A man took a step towards me, forcing me to look at him. "Heather Stone, right?"

"That's me."

He held up one of my flyers. "What happens at noon?"

"You'll have to stick around and find out."

"No hints?"

"No hints." I forced myself not to roll my eyes. I hoped he wouldn't stay to try to cajole the information out of me.

Of course, as Miss Lucy pointed out, all the commotion and interest in my story made people feel they had a claim on me. Almost as if the general population had adopted me.

I smirked to myself. Hopefully the general population formed strong bonds with their adopted relatives.

At five of twelve, I started making my way to the fountain in the center of the green. The clusters of people at the edges of the field were starting to stand up to make room for the people continuing to arrive. I had to shoulder my way through tightly packed bodies as I got closer to the fountain. I planned to use the raised stone wall around the tower of water as a platform.

My heart thudded against my rib cage, and I found myself wiping my hands against my skirt over and over again.

I will trust and not be afraid.

Halfway to my destination, I remembered my hat and pulled it off. The movement caught the attention of several people near the back.

As soon as they started pointing, progress became easier. People parted for me like the Red Sea parting for Moses. Conversations died to speculative whispers as I neared the fountain.

Even the whispering stopped when I climbed onto the fountain wall and everyone could see me.

For a second, my mind went completely blank. So many faces stared at me, waiting. After spending so much of my life trying to avoid attracting attention, it felt wrong to welcome it.

"Got something you want to tell us?" A man to my right asked.

"Yes, I do." I took a deep breath, squared my shoulders, and cleared my throat. "I have something I want to tell all of you." I spoke as loudly as I could.

Everyone remained quiet, watching, waiting, listening.

"I'm sure you all know that tomorrow afternoon my father will be executed."

This sent a ripple of conversation through the crowd.

"We don't know that," someone called. "He has the chance to recant."

I shook my head. "I know that tomorrow afternoon my father will be executed. I know this because I know my father will never recant. He would rather die."

Another burst of conversation. I paused until they quieted.

"The Bible tells us about many people like my dad," I told them. "The first Christian to die for his faith was a man named Stephen. He was stoned to death over two thousand years ago."

When I stopped for a breath, everyone stayed so quiet I could hear the leaves rustling in a slight breeze.

I continued. "Some men in the Bible got sentenced to death, but God miraculously saved them. One man, Daniel, lived in a country where a law was passed forbidding people to petition anyone besides the king for anything. The punishment for disobeying was being thrown into a den of angry lions."

I smiled a little as I scanned the crowd. This version of the story felt so normal, so simplified to me, yet my audience gave me their undivided attention.

"Daniel refused to sacrifice what he believed to protect his own safety," I told them, "so he continued to pray to God, and he made no effort to hide it."

People exchanged glances, shrugging at each other with expressions of confusion.

"God worked a miracle for Daniel." I took another deep breath, praying that God would help my words carry the impact I wanted them to. "Daniel was thrown into a den of lions, but God didn't allow the lions to eat Daniel. When the king called down to him the next morning, he answered and came out of the lions' den alive."

People smiled.

"What makes you think that story is true?" a woman several rows back shouted. "The government says the Bible is filled with fairy tales and lies."

"The government says that because the Bible has more power than they do, and they don't like that. I don't have any evidence to prove the truth of that story to you. Just like the government couldn't show you any proof that my Dad had the Bible they arrested him for owning."

"You're telling us Bible stories, though. So the government was right."

I nodded. "They were right. We did have that Bible. But they never found it. They didn't have any proof. And Daniel's story is true even though I can't prove it to you."

The women who had asked the question frowned but kept quiet.

"I'm praying for a miracle like Daniel got. I would love for God to prevent the government from killing my dad. That's the way I would like for God to prove to all of you that he's real."

People nodded their agreement.

"He might not do it that way, though," I said. "God might prove to you that He's real by showing you my Dad is willing to die rather than deny the truth of what he believes."

This time the nods came after a few seconds of hesitation. They were trying to understand. I smiled. That was a good sign. They weren't dismissing me. They were invested in trying to figure this out.

"If God wants to save my dad's life, he could very well work through you and me. That's what I want to ask of you. Please let the government know you want my Dad to live. You've read our story, and most of you sympathize with us. We don't want to start another rebellion. We simply want the government to return to us the freedom to practice our faith without fear of being arrested and executed for it."

More conversation made its way through the people. As I waited for it to die down, I caught a glimpse of uniformed men crossing the street and coming our way.

"Please," I shouted, "don't forget what you've read in our flyers and heard me say. You may not have evidence of governmental oppression, but we Christians have felt it."

I could sense the police getting closer and closer. My heart raced.

I struggled to keep my voice steady. "I felt the oppression when I watched the police shoot my mother. I've felt it as I've struggled through school, trying to keep up a false front to avoid having classmates turn me in."

Several policemen entered the far edges of the crowd. The outlying onlookers turned to watch them. I only had a few seconds left.

"A great man once said that the world will not be destroyed by those who do evil, but by those who watch and do nothing. Please don't be watchers."

I pressed a hand to my chest as people started clapping. A thrill of exhilaration bubbled through my fear. My plan was working. *Thank you, Lord.*

Seconds later, the uproar at the back of the crowd drew the attention of those closer to the center. People started turning around to watch the police. The uniformed men pushed through the crowd, coming towards me from every side.

I screamed in surprise as someone reached up and grabbed me. It was the man who'd asked for a hint earlier.

"You have to get out of here," he hissed.

I shook my head and tried to pull free. "I can't. Please."

"We'll help you." He grabbed my wrist and dragged me forward. "You can get away."

People pushed me from behind, urging me to go with him.

"No!" I cried. "You don't understand. I have to let them arrest me."

"Don't be ridiculous."

"You need to see this to make what I'm saying real to you."

I could see that he understood.

"It's an awfully big risk," he said.

"I know. But my dad has always taught me that death is only the beginning. I'm not afraid."

It was a lie. I was afraid. Terrified, but still determined as ever. I clenched my hands behind my back to keep them from shaking. What would they do to me?

This man was right. I could still run. The people would help me get away. I could buy myself more time and see what would happen.

But even as I weighed my options, I knew I couldn't run. I'd just asked all these people to stand firm and help me fight injustice. I couldn't turn tail after making that plea.

"You're sure?" the man asked.

I nodded.

He grabbed my hand and gave it a firm shake. "You're a brave girl, Heather Stone. We won't forget."

Chapter Eighteen

The crowd exploded into chaos as the police reached the fountain.

My self-appointed helper and several men he'd recruited struggled to keep frenzied civilians from dragging me away. The energy in the crowd reminded me of wind-whipped trees before a storm, ominous and warning of the approaching danger.

My little band of protectors scattered as the police reached us. For a second I found myself caught up in the raging storm. People grabbed at me, their hands closing around my wrists, my clothing, my hair. Too many of them for me to fight.

Someone jerked me back. I felt like I would be torn in two as the crowd and police fought over me. I tried to scream for them to stop but couldn't make myself heard.

More police swarmed forward, and the game of tug-o-war ended. The police enveloped me, forming a barrier against the crowd.

I crumpled, struggling to breathe. *God, please help me.*

A young officer dragged me to my feet and jerked my arms behind my back. He seemed almost as nervous as I was, but his roughness made me wince.

The crowd roared with indignation.

A hand appeared in my peripheral vision, and I flinched away before realizing it wasn't aimed at me. Instead it caught the young man on the side of the head.

He yelped and glared at the officer who had shoved him. "What was that for?"

"Don't rough the girl up." The officer turned to watch the crowd. "The last thing I want to deal with is a riot."

It's a little too late for that. The police barrier could just barely hold the crowd back. Every so often the people would surge forward and a policeman would stumble back, then spring forward to fill the gap.

When the young man finished handcuffing me, the officer called, "Let's move."

The cops created a triangular formation around us and started to forge a path through the crowd. I could feel the tension level rising among my escort. The angry crowd pressed against the human barrier, jostling them, pushing them, screaming at them. Several times we stopped moving all together.

The cacophony of voices swelled so loud I wished I could cover my ears. One voice broke through the rest, screaming my name. My heart skipped.

I scanned the crowd, searching for Bryce until I found him. He fought to maintain his position a row away from the line of police.

"Heather!" he screamed. Someone shoved him from behind and he stumbled forward, falling against one of the police. "Heather!"

We made eye contact, and I could see the panic in his expression. He didn't understand.

"It's okay," I said, knowing he couldn't hear me.

The police pushed him back, but he jumped forward again.

"What? Heather, what did you say?" The desperation in his voice felt like a knife stabbing into my heart.

I drew a deep breath. "It's okay!" I shouted.

The effect on the crowd was immediate. Everyone that could see or hear me froze. The silence rippled outward. For a moment, complete quiet reigned. Then a buzz of whispers rose from the crowd.

"What do you mean?" Bryce said. He spoke at a normal volume now, but I felt sure most of the crowd could hear him.

I scanned the mass of people, addressing everyone. "Fighting now will accomplish nothing. A riot will kill people and it will not save me.'"

The hum of whispers intensified.

"You have to let me go." I looked back at Bryce, holding his gaze and speaking directly to him.

His shoulders slumped. Tears glinted in his eyes. I forced back tears of my own. *Don't cry, Bryce. Please, don't cry.*

"Why?" He mouthed the word, meaning it only for me.

I shook my head at him. I could never explain from here. Not in this situation. I could only pray that my effort to shield him from guilt would work.

My escort started forward again. This time the crowd parted for them. The hush remained. An atmosphere of confusion surrounded us.

As we neared the edge of the crowd, I stopped and turned. The officer reached for my arm, then hesitated. I gave a wry smile. We both knew I had the upper hand. If he tried to stop me, the crowd would erupt again.

The people watched expectantly. To my surprise, I found Bryce still in the front line of the crowd.

My throat tightened. I felt tears on my cheeks and knew I wouldn't be able to say anything. This was goodbye.

I wanted to wave, but the handcuffs prevented me. It would be a silly gesture anyway. A salute would fit better. In lieu of both, I nodded.

Bryce put his hand over his chest. The people around him noticed the move and copied his symbol of respect and allegiance.

I raised my eyes towards the sky.

Bryce nodded. He understood. Allegiance to God must come before his love for me. I could only pray that God would give Bryce some sort of joy out of this sorrow.

Mom liked to say that God was close to the brokenhearted. Bryce certainly qualified. He was hunted by his biological father. Now he would probably lose both me and Dad, his adopted family. Unless, of course, Governor Williams surrendered to the pressure.

I surveyed the crowd again, amazed by the power I held over them. I had silenced hundreds of people with two simple words not even meant for them. There was still hope.

The police started forward again, and I went with them.

We reached the edge of the crowd and left it behind. I glanced over my shoulder to find everyone staring after us, hands over their hearts like a field of living statues.

They would not forget. They had listened to me. They had watched the government's response to what I said. They had seen how different that response was from their own.

Now I had to wait and see what they would do.

The police pushed me into the back of a car.

I leaned forward to make room for my cuffed hands and looked around. I had only been in a car once before, when I was little. I didn't remember much.

This car had tinted windows. A metal grate separated the front and back seats. I remembered reading about something similar in old police cars, but I never realized they still used them.

I tipped forward and rested my forehead against the grate. The adrenaline rushing out of my body left me feeling wobbly.

What now, Lord?

The officer and the young man who had handcuffed me climbed into the front seats.

"This is the problem with you Christian families," the officer said. "If we don't catch the parents soon enough, they brainwash the kids too."

"Dad didn't brainwash me." I forced my voice to stay even and neutral. "I made my own choice to follow Jesus, and I don't regret it."

He snorted as the car started moving. "That's what makes the brainwashing so scary. You think you made the choice yourself."

"Because it's true."

"Can't be." He shook his head. "It's easier to believe there's some well-refined brainwashing technique than to think so many people would be equally stupid."

"What makes us stupid?" I laced my fingers together, glad they couldn't see them trembling behind my back. "You think we're stupid just because we won't be bullied into giving up what we believe?"

The man glanced over his shoulder and glared at me. Apparently, he hadn't expected me to stand up to him.

I shrugged to myself. Why not? What more did I have to lose?

It didn't take long to arrive at the regional prison. I peered out the window as we drove up the long, winding driveway. The pictures didn't do it justice. The huge, squat building radiated a sense of foreboding.

Located at the top of a hill and separated from the city buildings, it seemed like an enemy fortress surveying its captured lands. The image wasn't far from the truth.

God, please, I prayed as the car pulled to a stop. *Help us know what to do. All of us.*

We needed guidance. I did. Dad did. Miss Lucy and Bryce and the underground church did. Even the supporters on the green needed God's help for the coming hours.

As the two men got out of the car, a verse whispered into my heart. *Take therefore no thought for the morrow: for the morrow shall take thought for the things of itself. Sufficient unto the day is the evil thereof.*

Sufficient evil indeed. More than sufficient, in fact.

The officer swung my door open and gestured for me to get out.

"We'll see how long you enjoy this game." He scowled and slammed the door shut behind me.

I didn't bother to tell him I didn't enjoy any of it and never had. A fire never went out if you kept feeding it.

The two men grabbed my arms and marched me toward the prison. I pushed my fear down, careful to keep my face blank.

The officer flashed a card at a guard by the gate.

The man hardly glanced at it. He pushed a button built into the wall and waved for us to go through the door.

My heart gave a little jump as they marched me inside. They pushed me against a height chart painted onto the cement wall. When they made the announcement about Dad, the picture of him had been taken in this very spot.

I stood still as they took my picture, but my hands were trembling again. Not from fear or nerves this time, but because Dad and I were under the same roof.

Another officer came out from behind a panel of one way glass and walked towards us.

"Heather Raziela Stone." He tapped a screen against his palm. "You've been causing us quite a bit of trouble."

"Yes, sir."

He frowned at me, and I knew why. Young people never addressed officials as sir or ma'am anymore.

"Did you really think you could get your father out of prison?"

"I hoped." I shrugged and lifted my chin. "I'm still hoping."

He slapped me. "Well stop. You don't have any hope left."

I met the man's gaze. "I wait for the Lord, my soul doth wait, and in his word do I hope."

"You'll be waiting a long time then." He scowled.

"No." I shook my head and reached for another verse. "Happy is he that hath the God of Jacob for his help, whose hope is the Lord his God."

"We didn't arrest you to get a Bible lesson. You'll learn to leave those fairy tales behind when reality hits."

"Reality?" My jaw tightened. How could anyone question my grip on reality? Old bitterness boiled up. I let a little of it escape in a tightly controlled manner. "I live in reality, sir. Reality was my mother dying and my father being arrested."

"Maybe your father being killed will finally do the job and teach you not to believe your magical stories."

"I don't believe in any fairy tales," I said. "I believe the verse that says 'Precious in the sight of the Lord is the death of his saints,' right along with the ones about hope and deliverance."

"Contradicting itself, then."

"No. Not at all. We have hope either way."

The man stared at me, then shook his head and waved impatiently at my captors. "Take her away."

They grabbed my arms and started across the room. We made it halfway across before he called us back.

The officer held his screen towards me. One of our posters filled the display. "Do you recognize this?"

"Of course."

He pointed to the handwritten location and time. "Then you recognize this as well."

"Yes, sir," I said. I knew what he was doing, but there seemed no point in denying it. "I wrote it myself."

"You realize that organizing, holding or supporting a public gathering of a religious nature is illegal?"

"Yes, sir. The same way owning a Bible and being a Christian is illegal. And I won't deny any of it."

"You're a fool."

"Let no man deceive himself," I quoted. "If any man among you seemeth to be wise in this world, let him become a fool, that he may be wise."

The man squinted at me.

I smiled, glad for the many hours spent memorizing verses. They steadied me. Rattling them off gave me something to focus on besides the gut-churning anxiety trying to gain full control of me.

"Yes, sir," I said, "I guess you would consider me a fool."

The expression on his face made me wish for a camera. I hoped anyone watching the security screens would enjoy it.

Thank you, Lord. I wanted to say it aloud but thought it best not to provoke the man unnecessarily.

"Don't you know what I can do to you?" he hissed. "To you and your father. Your life is in my hands."

The words sent a shiver down my spine. They were so close to what Pilate said to Jesus.

"You don't have any power over me at all," I said, Jesus' reply to Pilate running through my mind. I could quote it, but it seemed wrong for me to make the same claims Jesus had.

"Are you insane?" His voice rose in indignation. "Your father is to be killed tomorrow!"

"You can't do anything to either one of us unless God allows it." I willed my legs to hold me just a little longer. The calmness in my voice surprised me.

"You think your God is going to work a miracle for you," he spat the words like poison. "We had people in the crowd. We know."

"Daniel had three friends," I said. "They refused to bow down to a false god set up by their king. The king threatened their lives like you're threatening mine. Do you know what they said?"

"I don't. And I don't care to."

I ignored him. "They said that their God—who is my God as well—could save them from death and from the king. But if God chose not to save them, they would die without regret."

"And let me guess," he sneered, "they got rescued and lived happily ever after."

"Maybe not happily ever after, but God did rescue them, yes."

"Like I said, fairy tales. You won't get rescued. The government is stronger than God."

I shook my head, looking him in the eye. "I believe you'll live to regret that statement. Remember your history lesson about the Titanic? People said even God couldn't sink that ship."

"Nice try, but that was a long time ago."

I smiled at him, surprised that I could. Inside I felt sick from fear and uncertainty.

"Tell me," I said, "if what I'm saying doesn't make you a little bit nervous and curious, why are you standing here arguing with a prisoner?"

He stared at me again. Then he snapped his gaze away from me. "Take her away. I'll deal with her later."

Chapter Nineteen

My legs finally buckled as they threw me into my cell.

I crawled to one of the back corners of the cell and pulled my knees up to my chest. Pain seared from my temples, through my head, and down my neck.

Please help Bryce understand, I prayed. *Don't let him hurt too much.*

I closed my eyes and rested my forehead against my knees. The throbbing made me feel nauseated. I stifled a moan. No doubt some kind of security camera was watching me. I didn't want them to think they had won.

Tears pressed against my eyelids.

I blew out a long breath and stretched out on the cool stone floor. The cold felt good against my head.

Maybe I could think of a way to get them to let me see Dad before his meeting tomorrow. Maybe I wouldn't even have to ask. They might hope that seeing me in prison would make Dad rethink his decision.

If one of us recanted, the government would have what it wanted. The threat we presented would diffuse, and they wouldn't have to worry. They would push for that outcome.

The brisk clip of footsteps reverberated through the floor, knifing through my aching head. I sat up, pressing a hand over my mouth as my stomach roiled.

The man from upstairs swung the cell door open.

"You have three days." He threw a piece of paper at me. It fluttered to the floor.

I picked it up and scanned the official letterhead. It was the official announcement for my Recanting Meeting.

"Dad's meeting tomorrow, a day in between for me to think, and then mine?"

"Precisely." He seemed pleased.

"I'd like to talk to him."

The man snickered. "How nice."

"I want his help in choosing my answer."

"I see." He shook his head, a glimmer of amusement in his eyes. "You can talk to him tomorrow."

"What do you mean?"

"You'll find out soon enough, Heather." He laughed and stepped out of the cell. "Sleep well and say your prayers. You'll need all the help you can get."

Anxious curiosity made me fight sleep, but exhaustion won out. I didn't even realize I'd fallen asleep until I woke up.

The harsh light coming from a single bare light bulb made me think it was morning. Then I remembered capitol buildings could store energy, so I couldn't guess the time after all.

The last of my headache remained as stabbing pricks of pain around the edges of my temples. Nothing too severe, and my stomach felt much better.

I wondered what the officer had meant when he said I could talk to Dad today.

Eventually, a guard delivered breakfast, and I knew it was morning.

I picked at the rubbery eggs and fermented juice, not tasting what little I ate. Morning meant the countdown had begun in earnest. Only a few hours remained until Dad's Recanting Meeting.

I wished I knew what was going on outside the prison walls.

The apprehension of ignorance threatened to overwhelm me as more time passed. I knew that what felt like hours were probably only minutes.

The guard took my breakfast away.

To keep them from shaking, I sat on my hands until they ached. I prayed as hard as I ever had in my life. Sometimes my mind couldn't even form words, but my heart kept crying out in a way my mind could never match.

And then he came for me. The officer from the previous day. Instead of the everyday uniform he'd worn before, he now wore a dress uniform. It made him look stiff and, from the robotic way he moved, I guessed he didn't feel very comfortable in it.

"You are to come with me," he said.

I got up and followed him out of the cell and down a long, tunnel-like hallway. "Where are we going?"

"You'll find out soon enough." He wasted no time taunting or arguing today.

"What time is it?"

He glanced at me and smirked. "I thought you would have guessed by now."

That gave me the hint I needed. It was time for the Recanting Meeting. They must want me to watch it. I wondered if they would put me in a room with a screen or have me in the same room to watch it live.

I remembered the man telling me I could talk to Dad today and decided they meant for me to watch it live. I wondered if we'd have a chance to talk.

"You know," he said in a conversational tone, "that announcement about your Recanting Date hasn't been made public yet."

I didn't respond. No point in biting the bait he laid out. If he wanted to tell me, he would do so without my asking.

He glared at me. "Fine, Miss High-and-Mighty, you can wait to find out why we haven't. Let it be a surprise."

Despite the situation, I fought the impulse to roll my eyes. How juvenile could a grown man get? How on earth did a bunch of people like this run a country?

I recognized the Recanting Room as soon as we stepped into it. We didn't own a television, but I'd seen reruns on public screens.

Three chairs sat at the far end of the rectangular room, set in front of a black cloth backdrop. Two cameras on either side of the door focused on the chairs.

I eyed them nervously. There should only be two chairs, one for Dad and one for the Chief of Police.

I took a deep breath. If people cared the way I intended them to, the government would risk another rebellion if they executed Dad.

I glanced at the officer standing behind me and winced. Would people like him even realize that? Bullies didn't seem to weigh the consequences of their actions. They assumed they could force people into submission through superior strength alone.

The officer pushed me towards a chair against the right wall. "You've got a few minutes. Wait there."

I sat down and tried not to fidget. When I realized willpower alone would not keep my hands still, I finger combed my hair and started braiding it. If they meant to make me part of the show, I might as well look presentable.

It took three tries to make the braid come out right. Not a good sign when it usually took me one try and a grand total of thirty-seconds. Just as I finished twisting a hair elastic from my wrist onto the end of the braid, the door opened again. Two guards entered, one in front, one behind, and Dad in the middle.

I shrieked and jumped out of my chair. I didn't care what they did to me. Darting forward, I flung my arms around Dad.

He'd lost weight and several dark bruises stood out against the pale skin on his face and arms. As soon as his arms closed around me, I forgot about everything else and started crying.

"Daddy, I missed you so much."

He rested his cheek against the top of my head for a second, then kissed me. "I missed you too, sweetheart."

"I've tried everything I could think of to get you out of this. We've been..."

"Shh." He kissed the top of my head. "I know. You've been amazing."

I cried harder. I didn't know how he knew what I'd been doing, but I didn't care. It didn't matter.

When the guards pulled us apart, it felt like they were jerking my heart out. I choked back sobs that threatened to become hysterical. I needed to be strong.

Dad eased himself into one of the chairs at the end of the room and smiled at me.

I could read every bit of meaning behind the smile. He was telling me to be strong. To not worry about him. That God was in control and would take care of us.

I started to sit back down, but the officer stopped me.

"No." He pointed towards Dad. "You're to sit next to him now."

I obeyed, trying to guess what they meant to do. Did they intend to create a double Recanting Meeting?

Dad reached over and squeezed my hand.

I squeezed back, then laced my fingers between his. It felt so good to be together with Dad again. Whatever they had planned, we could do it together.

The Chief of Police stomped through the door a few moments later. He stopped between the cameras and surveyed the room.

I tried to remember his name. Chief Hedgepole or something like that. Hedgepole wasn't quite right, but it was as close as I could get.

"Everything is ready, sir," the officer said.

"Good." Hedgepole crossed the room and sat down on my other side. He peered at his watch. "Going live in thirty seconds."

Thirty seconds? I sucked in a quick breath and Dad squeezed my hand again. I squeezed back, forcing myself to breathe steady and slow.

I will trust and not be afraid.

The camera men moved into position. One of them started a countdown. "Going live in five, four, three, two and action."

Hedgepole stared at the cameras for a full five seconds before turning towards us. I instinctively leaned away from him.

The man smirked and looked back at the cameras.

"As I'm sure you know, our guests today are Rayford and Heather Stone. Both of them are Christian rebels."

I glanced at Dad and found him staring straight into the cameras. I smiled a little and copied him. I wondered if the man from the green was watching.

"Both of them have admitted to adhering to the Christian faith, owning Bibles, and participating in Christian gatherings. All of these are illegal activities punishable by death."

A verse from Romans popped into my head. *As it is written, for thy sake we are killed all the day long; we are accounted as sheep for the slaughter.*

I swallowed hard. *I'm willing, Lord. Truly I am. Just help me be strong.*

And then I remembered the next verse. *Nay, in all these things we are more than conquerors through him that loved us.*

I lifted my chin and allowed a tiny smile to creep onto my face. A smile that told the world I had a secret. A smile that told them I had something the government could never take away.

"As a government that cares for its people, we are willing to give the Stones an opportunity to recant their silly beliefs. If they do, we will offer them a pardon and the continued goodwill of the government."

My heart pounded, but I kept the smile fixed on my face. What did they have in mind? I wanted to do away with the suspense and find out, yet at the same time I dreaded knowing.

"We realize," Hedgepole continued, "that most of our viewers did not expect to see Miss Stone on today's broadcast. Most of you know the rumors of her arrest, but no official announcement has been made."

Which meant they were leading up to something. They wanted as much of a surprise factor as possible.

"Well, as you can see, the rumors are true. Miss Stone was arrested while inciting a crowd to revolt."

I smirked into the cameras, wondering how many people would believe the lie. The people who had been there would recognize the falsehood. With so many witnesses, the government was sure to snare itself within its web of deceit this time.

He forged on, unaware of the foolishness of his statement. "We are aware that many of you watching have become quite sympathetic to Miss Stone. And, because of her, to her father as well. You know that her desire is to see her father released."

All true, but it did nothing to put me at ease.

Dad squeezed my hand again, then, after a hesitation, put his arm around me.

I leaned against him, smiling for real but fighting tears at the same time. Willing or not, I didn't want to lose him. The very thought made the tears escape and roll down my cheeks.

Dad rubbed his thumb over my shoulder.

"Because Miss Stone has been so active in trying to secure his release," he smiled into the camera, "and because all of you seem to support her in this desire, we have decided to give her the opportunity to ensure his freedom."

Dad's arm tightened around me.

I wondered if he knew their plan. Maybe he had guessed it. Or maybe he knew as little as I did but assumed it couldn't be good.

"We hope you will agree that this is a generous arrangement and leaves his fate entirely in Miss Stone's hands."

Just tell us what the arrangement is already.

"We have decided to allow Miss Stone to speak for her father in this Recanting Meeting."

Chapter Twenty

My heart sank. I knew what I had to do. I could never recant. Not for myself and not for Dad. My answer cemented itself in my mind the moment Hedgepole spoke, but knowing and doing were two entirely different matters.

"Sweetheart," Dad breathed. He closed his eyes and tipped his head against mine.

I leaned into him, expecting them to force us apart at any moment. I trembled like a fall leaf, blown by the wind but still clinging to the tree.

I will trust and not be afraid.

But I was afraid. Afraid of what I had to do. Afraid that if I gave the answer I had to, people would think I'd blown my chance to free Dad.

Were they pressuring the president now? Was all this a bluff? Was it staged to make a declaration of mercy all the more dramatic?

What if this was the bargain the governor had struck with the people? What if their protests had led to this decision? What if this was my only chance?

Hedgepole turned to look at me.

I forced myself to stop crying. Tightening my jaw, I sat up straight and tried to stop shivering.

"Miss Stone," he said, "we ask you to speak on behalf of your father. With the knowledge that your faith is illegal in this country and punishable by death, will Rayford Stone recant? If he does, a full pardon will be granted immediately. If not he will die by lethal injection."

I reached for Dad's hand, and he squeezed it.

God, please help us.

When I glanced at Dad, he nodded.

I turned back to Hedgepole and took a deep breath. "Yesterday, I told the people on the green about two people sentenced to death for their faith. One was miraculously saved. The other died. Neither one renounced their faith. They let God decide the results."

"No sermons please, Miss Stone," he droned. He looked ready to fall asleep.

"I know what my father's answer would be today, so I will speak on his behalf." I took another deep breath. I couldn't keep speaking. My chest ached, and a lump in my throat threatened to choke me.

I need Your strength, Lord.

"Sweetheart," Dad murmured. He knew. He knew how hard this was. But we had only one option.

I turned away from Hedgepole and buried my face against Dad's shoulder, unable to hold back a wrenching sob.

He put a hand against the back of my head and stroked my hair. "Shhh. Sweetheart. It's okay. I love you."

I felt Hedgepole's hand on my shoulder. Dad pushed it away. I expected them to summon guards to force us to cooperate, then realized they didn't want my decision to seem forced. The population of our small corner of the world was watching.

Dad held me for a little longer, then gently pushed me away. He cupped my face between his hands. "Be strong and courageous," he whispered, "be not afraid or dismayed."

I dried my eyes, then gave him a tight hug before turning to face the cameras.

"I cannot and will not recant anything," I quoted, my voice steady though tears continued flooding down my face. "Here I stand, I can do no other, so help me God."

Silence reigned for several seconds before Dad's hand closed on my shoulder. "I would not have wished her to say anything else."

Hedgepole glared at us for a second before catching himself. "Are you sure, Miss Stone?"

I nodded.

"Very well." He turned to the cameras. "I hope our viewers will be satisfied that the government has done all it can to offer the Stones forgiveness and pardon."

My heart dropped. I had failed again. Utterly and completely failed. Desperation raged inside me, clawing and piercing my heart.

A doctor came through the door, dressed in a white lab coat and carrying a syringe. Governor Williams accompanied him.

Dad and I tensed.

God, no. Please no.

There was still time for the governor to change his mind. Someone could call him to report chaos in the streets and angry citizens demanding Dad's life be spared.

The officer stepped forward and reached for me.

"No!" I didn't mean to shriek, but all the agony in my heart came out with the word.

Dad's hand tightened on my shoulder, telling me to stay strong.

"Please," I said in a more controlled tone, "let me stay."

Hedgepole hesitated, then smiled at Governor Williams. "What do you say, governor?"

I could tell he was relieved to have a superior present to defer to.

"She can stay," the governor said tersely.

"You have a fine son," Dad said, lifting his chin to catch the governor's attention.

Safely off camera, the man scowled. His efforts to hide his son's faith had just been ruined.

"What happened to you?" Dad asked. "At one time you would have died rather than allow injustice like this."

Hedgepole and the doctor both seemed uncertain. The cameramen glanced from us, to the governor, and back again. They started turning the cameras to include the governor in the shot, then stopped.

"I'm not allowing any injustice."

"No?" Dad raised his eyebrows. "If you're not allowing it, you're orchestrating it."

"Not orchestrating either. There is no injustice. You and your religion destroyed this country."

Dad shook his head. "Not me. I was too young to fight, just like you."

"Your religion, then," the governor hissed.

"This country was built on my religion," Dad said. "Christianity made it strong. Immorality caused it to crumble."

"That's what I can't stand about you." The governor stepped forward, into the line of the cameras. The cameramen exchanged uncertain glances. "Your holier-than-thou attitude, thinking everyone else is destroying the world and your religion can fix everything."

"Both sides were equally responsible for the war." Dad remained calm, but I could see the pain in his eyes. "If you could look back with an unbiased eye, you would see that, Reed."

"Governor Williams."

"I've called you Reed since we were boys. I'm not going to change that minutes before I die."

Don't say that. Oh, please, don't say that.

"You brainwashed my son."

"Your son came to me with questions," Dad said.

Governor Williams scowled. "You'll never change your mind, will you?"

Dad shook his head. "Never. Though He slay me, yet will I trust him."

The governor's eyes hardened. "Your God won't slay you. I will."

The doctor took that as his cue and stepped forward.

"No, please," I cried. I couldn't hold it back. "Please, don't."

"Shut up." The governor glared at me. "You had your chance."

"She never had a choice," Dad said. "Recanting was never an option, and she knew it." He held up his hand to ask the doctor to wait. "Give us a moment."

The doctor hesitated, and Dad wrapped his arms around me.

I clung to him, sobbing. "Daddy, I can't do this. I can't."

"Yes, you can." He smoothed my hair. "Death is only the beginning. I'm not afraid."

"But I am, Daddy. I'm so afraid."

"Of dying?"

"No," I sobbed. "I'm afraid of you dying."

He kissed my forehead. "Don't be."

I started shaking again, but this time I didn't try to stop. "Please Daddy."

"It's okay," he said. "I'll fall asleep and wake up in Heaven. It's not a bad way to go."

"But I still need you."

"No." He shook his head. "God wouldn't take me if you needed me."

Governor Williams cleared his throat.

"It's time, sweetheart." Dad brushed the tears off my cheeks with his thumbs, then used his forefinger to tip my chin up. "He hath said, I will never leave thee nor forsake thee."

Dad pushed his left sleeve up, then laced the fingers of his right hand together with mine.

The panic threatened to conquer my common sense. I fought for control. I needed to be strong, for Dad and for the people watching. The same as Dad was being strong for me.

"Last words?" Hedgepole asked.

Dad nodded. He looked straight into the camera on the right as he spoke. "The wicked is driven away in his wickedness: but the righteous hath hope in his death. We are confident, I say, and willing rather to be absent from the body, and to be present with the Lord."

I recognized both verses. My mind searched for the references out of habit. Proverbs 14:32 and 2 Corinthians 5:8.

Dad stiffened as the doctor slid the needle into his arm.

The room swam in front of my eyes. I closed my eyes and screamed a silent prayer. *Don't let me pass out. Please, God. Please. Please. Please.*

Dad squeezed my hand yet again.

I opened my eyes and looked at him through a film of tears. When I blinked, they rolled down my face and my vision cleared for a split second before more tears welled up to take their place.

When Dad spoke, his voice was quiet, the words meant only for me. "I love you, sweetheart. I'll see you again."

"I love you too, Daddy." I shook with silent sobs. "I'll be counting the days."

The drugs were working fast. I could feel his fingers weakening.

"Psalm 138:3," he whispered.

My brain wouldn't work and I didn't try to make it. "I'll remember."

He gave a little gasp. "Tell Bryce I love him. I love you, sweetheart."

"I know, Daddy. I love you too."

I waited for him to say more, but he didn't.

Chapter Twenty-One

The tears blinded me, but I didn't need to see to tell when it ended. The life drained from the fingers still intertwined with mine.

Dad slumped in his chair.

I didn't scream, but sobs seized my entire body as I clung to his hand.

An image flashed across my mind. Dad coming home and learning that Mom was dead. He had clutched her bloodied ID cards and screamed.

When a guard stepped forward to take Dad away, I revived a little. I tightened my fingers around his hand, refusing to let go. They couldn't take him away. Not again.

But when the officer pried my hand away from Dad's, I stopped resisting. I slid off my chair and crumpled on the floor. I wrapped my arms around my stomach and curled my body around them.

"Up." The officer grabbed my arm and hauled me to my feet.

I stumbled after him as he pulled me down the corridor. I tripped several times, but his grip on my arm kept me upright.

Back in my cell I huddled in the corner, no longer worried about looking strong for the security camera. My own Recanting Meeting could not come soon enough. And yet the thought of it terrified me.

My mind kept replaying the scene in the Recanting Room over and over again until it finally focused on one of the last things Dad had said. *Psalm 138:3.*

What was Psalm 138:3? Dad knew I didn't have a Bible available so he must have thought I would know it.

The focus required to think of the verse helped me gain control of myself. The wrenching sobs ended.

My head throbbed as I forced it to think. What was Dad's last message to me?

It took a while, but I finally remembered. *In the day when I cried thou answeredst me, and strengthenedst me with strength in my soul.*

"Heather?"

I groaned as the urgent whisper penetrated my sleep.

"Heather, you've got to wake up."

I forced my eyes open. They burned and stung from the hours of crying, and the persistent headache remained.

"Heather? Heather, listen to me."

I pushed myself into a sitting position as I recognized the voice. It was Bryce.

He fumbled with a stack of cards, waving them one at a time across the wall next to my door. When he found the right one, the lock clicked open.

"What are you doing here?" I hissed. "Where did you get those?"

"Preventing a war, that's what I'm doing."

"How did you get in here? Where did you get those cards?" I scrambled to my feet.

Bryce grinned and pushed the door open. "I've still got Dad's ID card. I snitched the key cards from his office. He's busy with the press."

I stared at him, trying to make the whirlwind of information make sense.

"Can't explain now." He grabbed my hand and pulled me through the door, glancing at the security camera. "The prison is having unexplained difficulty with the security system, but we can't count on it to last."

My mind spun as I allowed him to drag me down the corridor.

With the events of the past forty-eight hours still crushing me, my brain felt too muddled to do anything except obey.

Why hadn't Bryce done this yesterday and rescued me *and* Dad? *God, why?*

To my surprise, when we got outside, Bryce pulled me towards a government car, pushed me inside and toppled in after me.

"Go!" he gasped.

The car lurched into motion as the driver shifted into gear and pulled onto the long driveway.

"What is going on?" I demanded. "How did you get in there? I don't understand."

"The city is going crazy, Heather." Bryce nudged me over so that we could both sit in our seats instead of sprawling across the back of the car. "The Recanting Meetings shown on the screen in the past were recorded and edited before they went live."

I didn't know that. I thought back to some of the ones I had seen. That would explain why people never seemed to make a strong profession of their faith, even when they consented to die for it.

"You said most." I glanced at him. "Dad's was different?"

Bryce nodded. "The network has been working like mad. We got Christians into the television hub, and they switched things around so the feed from the Recanting Room played live."

"What happened?"

"The city erupted. People are furious. There were riots all night. Not just here either. They brought in military from other regions to try to keep things quiet, but the broadcast showed across the country, so it's spreading."

I took a few minutes to process that. Swallowing hard, I whispered, "It wasn't in vain."

"What's that?" Bryce tilted his head closer to mine.

"It wasn't in vain," I said, trying yet again to hold back tears. "Dad dying. It wasn't, wasn't in..."

I couldn't continue, but I didn't need to.

Bryce scooted over and put his arm around me. "I'm so sorry, Heather."

I put my head against his shoulder and let myself cry again.

Bryce rubbed my back. He didn't try to say anything, just let me cry. After the long, lonely hours of grieving alone in my cell, the comfort of having someone who cared felt like a heaven-sent gift.

"He said to tell you he loved you, Bryce," I said when I could talk again. "He wanted you to know."

"I already knew."

When I looked up, I found Bryce's face also wet with tears.

"I failed, Bryce."

"No," he said, his voice fierce, "you didn't fail. You didn't get the result you wanted, but you achieved everything your dad wanted and more.'"

"He's dead."

"I know." He gave me another squeeze. "Except a corn of wheat fall into the ground and die..."

I nodded and finished the verse. "It abideth alone: but if it die, it bringeth forth much fruit."

We sat in silence for a while.

"It doesn't make losing him easier," I said.

"I know it doesn't."

"But maybe it does a little bit."

"We're going to make it." Bryce squeezed my shoulder and managed a smile. "You ready to keep fighting?"

"Not really." I wiped my cheeks and took a deep breath. "But at the same time, I've never been more ready in my life."

"Good. Because we went all out while you were gone."

I raised my eyebrows in question.

"One of our members made another full-sized press." He grinned. "And we pulled a little raid on the government's paper warehouse."

I stared at him. "You did what?"

"We wanted to be prepared."

I smiled. I knew exactly what I wanted to write.

Bryce was right. Our city teetered on the brink of war. We got through several police and military barricades only because of the government insignia on our car.

The change seemed an almost tangible force.

I frowned, confused when the driver turned down a narrow side road and braked.

"Come on." Bryce grabbed my hand again and pulled me out of the car.

"I don't recognize this place. Did something change?" I couldn't imagine moving our headquarters into the city. "Did something happen to the Greens?"

"The Greens are fine." Bryce nodded at the car. "Government vehicles aren't being kindly received by the general population today. People will be much happier to see you."

I ran my hands over my rumpled blouse and skirt, then touched my face. My eyes must be bloodshot from all the crying. And, worse, I knew it wouldn't take much to make me cry again.

"I'm not sure I'm ready to see anyone," I said.

Bryce smiled. "You'll do fine. Everyone will understand. They saw everything yesterday."

"You kept showing the feed after Dad died?"

He nodded. "Why wouldn't we? Your breakdown touched people in a way they're not used to."

"They don't blame me for his death?"

"Some might, but the majority doesn't." He started back towards the main road. "Watching your story made a lot of people realize how wrong the Recanting Meeting's are."

I nodded. I couldn't believe I'd never realized the Recanting Meetings were edited.

We walked in silence for a while. Despite the precaution taken by not driving the government vehicle into the city, the streets seemed unusually empty. Instead of the normal sound of people talking and the occasional whine of a car, I could hear only our footsteps and birds singing.

And then I saw the graffiti—if you could even call it that—spray painted on the middle of the road in white letters.

"Bryce, look!" I grabbed his arm and pointed.

He looked and grinned. "I know. Stuff like that is everywhere."

I stood and stared. The words on the road said, "He hath said, I will never leave thee nor forsake thee."

"There are Bible verses all over the city," Bryce said. "It started even before the Recanting Meeting. People at the green were furious when you got arrested."

I shook my head. "I feel like the world changed while I was in prison."

"It has." Bryce grinned and pulled me after him. "Your recanting quote is everywhere too. And we've been pushing Bible passages onto public datasites too. The government finds them and wipes them, but we just repost."

"What do you mean?"

"I mean, not all the verses you'll see are ones you and your dad said on television."

"People have changed their minds about religion just like that?"

Bryce shrugged. "I don't think most of these people ever had an opinion on it. They just didn't think about it at all. Didn't even know about it."

"And they just accepted it? Just like that?"

"You and your questions." Bryce chuckled. "I wouldn't assume everyone suddenly got saved. But they're not apathetic anymore." There was excitement in his voice. "They've all been padded into their safe, comfortable little world and all of a sudden you showed them injustice and made them care about someone else."

"Never thought it would turn into this." I pointed at another Bible verse written onto the street. John 3:16 this time.

Bryce stopped.

I turned around. "What?"

"Shhh." He put his hand up. "Do you hear something?"

"No." I frowned, listening. And then I did hear it. The tramping of feet and a growing murmur of voices.

"That's either military or another mob," Bryce said.

We started searching for a place to hide, but the storefronts stretched on either side of the road for quite a ways without a break.

"We'll have to find a doorway and hope for the best." I started across the street, heading for the doorway to a shop with a metal curtain pulled over its windows.

"I think it's too late," Bryce said.

I hesitated in the middle of the road and looked up to find a swarm of people turning the corner ahead of us and coming into view. No question they could see us.

"At least it's a mob instead of military." Bryce joined me. "I think that's a good thing. They're more inclined to like you."

We stayed in the middle of the street, watching and waiting. I tried to plan what to do or say if they recognized me, but my brain refused to come up with anything.

When the people got close enough for those in the front to see my face, the buzz of conversation started growing. It got louder and louder until a man separated himself from the group and hollered at them to be quiet.

To my surprise, everyone listened.

"Might be a mob, but it's an awfully tame one," I muttered to Bryce.

He nodded.

The man leading the crowd jogged towards us, pulling his hat off as he approached. It was the man from the green, the one who asked me for a hint and tried to help me run away from the police. The one who promised not to forget.

"Hi," I said when he stopped in front of us. It sounded as awkward as it felt.

"I'm so sorry about your dad," he said. "We tried. I think ninety-five percent of the people in that crowd told everyone they knew what had happened as soon as you left."

"Thanks." I took a deep breath and forced myself not to think too long about Dad. "We both appreciate it. Me and Dad, I mean."

He nodded. "We didn't forget."

"I know. I've been seeing the verses all over the place."

He gestured at the people behind him. "We heard you were getting out of prison. We've been looking for you. We want to know what we can do to help."

"How did you know...?" I trailed off without finishing the sentence. It didn't really matter. I glanced past him and studied the crowd. "You brought an army with you."

"Your army." He smiled. "I know you said you didn't intend to start a rebellion, but rebellion or no, you've started a war."

And he was right. I had started a war. Or maybe God had started a war through me. A war against principalities and powers and evil in high places.

Deep down inside a flicker of hope started burning again. This fledgling army reminded me that someday we would win the war once and for all. There would be casualties. More casualties. But even a conquering army had casualties.

I smiled. Death was only the beginning of the story. Every single person looking back at me carried a bit of Dad with them. The corn had fallen into the ground and died, but it was bringing forth much fruit.

I walked forward until I stood half way between Bryce and the crowd. They stared at me expectantly

I lifted one fist above my head. "Be strong and courageous!" I shouted the words, Dad's final admonition to me. I would carry them in my heart forever, and I would share them with the world. "We will not forget!"

The crowd roared the words back at me, and I knew that together we would carry Dad's legacy. We would not let him die in vain. I would keep my promise and run the race set before me.

And I would not run alone.

Acknowledgements

Many thanks to the Kickstarter partners who helped Counted Worthy reach its full potential. Each of these folks was part of the project that transformed Counted Worthy from a manuscript to a book. Here's a round of grateful applause for Christopher Kingsley, The Clifford Family, Edward Sarabia, Grant Lincoln, Heather Hufford, Jay & Crystal van Achterberg, Jesse Schroeder, Jonathan K. Good, Joshua Bayless, Joyous Penn, Kelsey Zink, Kenneth J. Good, Lindsey Caton, Lisi Ferg, Madison Woodard, MaryEmma Hughes, Melody van Achterberg, Michael Farrar, Miguel Flores, Samantha Black, Shari Austin, Spencer J Rothfuss, Sue Lynch, Susan E. Good, The Turner Family, TW Wright, and Zechariah Stover.

Thanks also to the many people who have encouraged, taught, and believed in this writing dream over the past five years. My writing buddies—Hannah Mills, Lindsey Caton, Rachel Garner, and Pamela Kask—who have patiently critiqued many manuscripts. Daniel Schwabauer, who wrote the curriculum that got me on the path to writing well. My parents, who encouraged me, paid for most of my writing education, and gave me the freedom to focus on bringing this book to publication. Thanks to Brett Harris for taking the time to promote the Kickstarter campaign, read the manuscript, and give a budding author some much appreciated confidence. Thanks to my very first fan, my brother Jonathan. And last but not least, a special thanks to Marli Renee for using her artistic talent to bring Heather Stone to life for this non-visual writer.

There are many other people who could be acknowledged. If you're one of them, know that you're appreciated. Thank you.